I0760697

The Black Badge

Confessions of Corruption

By

C.L. Lowry

Creedom Publishing Company
Philadelphia, Pennsylvania

This book is a work of fiction. Names, characters, places, and incidents either are products of the author's imagination or are used fictitiously. Any resemblance to actual persons, living or dead, events, or locales is entirely coincidental.

The Cataloging-in-Publication Data is on file at the Library of Congress.

Creedom Publishing Company

Visit the websites at
www.CreedomPublishing.com
www.TheBlackBadge.com

ISBN-13: 978-1-946897-92-3
ISBN-10: 1-946897-92-2
LCCN: 2016900737

Printed in the United States of America
11 10 9 8 7 6 5 4 3 2

Acknowledgements

I would like to thank the following people for their continuous help and support:

To my fiancé, thank you for tolerating the long nights of listening to my planning the release of this novel. Also, thank you for supporting me every time I approach you with a new endeavor. Words can't explain how great it's to have your love and support.

To my children, thank you for all the encouragement and countless hours of listening to my ideas to develop a way to allow the world to read my work.

To my family, there has never been a time when you all haven't had my back. I could count on each and every one of you if I ever ran into hard times and I am truly grateful for that.

To my friends, you all are more like family. Whether it was listening to my crazy ideas or giving me constructive feedback on stories, you all have been there throughout this entire strenuous process. We started out as young mischievous children from the mean streets of Philly and have developed into beacons of hope for our communities. We must continue to strive to inspire the world.

Last but not least, I'd like to thank the readers of this novel. A lot of hard work goes into writing a book like this and I hope that is reflected in my writing. We as people must get back to the days when we would help and support each other. These stories were not written tarnish the badge of our brave men and women, but instead to shine a lot on the lack of support for most of them. They are humans too and we all make mistakes. I hope you enjoy.

Table of Contents

Introduction

Police is defined as an organized civil force for maintaining order, preventing and detecting crime, and enforcing the law. Being a police officer is a very dangerous and serious career choice. The position gives men and women the authority to change lives. This authority demands a great amount of responsibility. There are high expectations that need to be met by every officer, that do not come with a lot of reward. When gunshots are fired, police officers are expected to run towards them, while everyone else runs away. When someone is in danger, a police officer is expected to put their life on the line to protect and preserve another. When someone needs help, police officers are expected to be the solution to their problem. Police officers are supposed to be role models before they are anything else. They are looked upon as a positive entity in a negative world and models of perfection that should do no wrong. When they wear their badges, they are to put their own personal issues aside to deal with everyone else's... and this burden can become very heavy over time.

Now as hard as it's being a police officer in general, imagine being one in a major city such as Philadelphia. Being an officer in the City of Brotherly Love is an experience like no other. An experience that cannot be described in mere words, not even by the men and women who do the job every day. What many police departments deal with in ten years, Philadelphia Police deal with in a month. What many police officers witness in their entire twenty to thirty year careers, a Philadelphia police officer sees in a year or less. What for many departments is a rare call to respond to "shots fired," Philly cops often have to run towards them three or four times in an eight hour tour of duty. The call for help, domestic disturbance or large bar fight occurs so often during a tour of duty that it can be physically and emotionally overwhelming. Not only do the officers deal with the citizen's problems daily, but they have to handle their own once they are off duty. To take on the responsibility to protect someone leaves an officer in situations they never imagined they would be in. But to take on the responsibility of protecting the citizens of Philadelphia leaves some officers with the brutal reality that they have lost their purity and innocence. The same purity and innocence that made them take an oath to protect and serve.

This great responsibility changes some officers. The burdens in their personal lives can take over and the job itself can consume them. In a city plagued with violence and crime, officers who once put on their badges and wore them with pride now find themselves on the opposite end of the law. Often, officers lose their morals and can no longer be trusted. The light that a police officer shines suddenly gets dark. The emotion a child feels when they are around a police officer turns from trust to fear. The shining badge an officer wears on their chest to represent honor, integrity, and service, suddenly darkens through deception, corruption and greed. These are the stories of officers who have worn *THE BLACK BADGE.*

CHAPTER ONE

As an eighteen-year veteran of the Philadelphia Police Department, Lieutenant Sandra Smith was no stranger to danger, but she never expected the random act of fate that would change her life forever.

Sandra began her career as a patrol officer in Philadelphia's 6th District, which covers the Center City section of Philadelphia. After only seven years as an officer, she was promoted to sergeant. Just eight years later, she made lieutenant. The whole time she climbed the ranks, Sandra managed to be a loving wife and mother to her four children. While responding to a bank robbery in the spring of 2011, Sandra was involved in a major car crash. As a result of the crash, Sandra suffered a severe back injury. Dealing with that impairment changed not only her career, but her life.

This is Lieutenant Sandra Smith's story...

PAIN

Since I was a little girl, I always wanted to be a police officer. I grew up in the South Philadelphia area of the city, but had a pretty normal childhood. After earning a Master's Degree in Criminal Justice from Temple University, I never had any doubt what to do next. I knew my calling was to serve the city I grew up in, so I immediately enrolled in the police academy. I had a fabulous career and was able to raise a beautiful family at the same time.

Sure, I had certain physical setbacks during my career, due to receiving epidural shots when I gave birth to each of my four children. These shots left me with occasional back pain, which was no minor inconvenience in my line of work. The strain on my back worsened every time I wore my duty belt. Just imagine wearing forty to fifty pounds of equipment around your waist, five days a week for eighteen years straight. Some days at work were just brutal, but I pushed through the pain and never let it cripple me.

I tried so many products to help support my back while on duty, but nothing seemed to be a long-term solution. It probably didn't help that I was philosophically opposed to taking any type of medication. Over the years, I saw several doctors and specialists that were all very persistent that medication was the only way to deal with my back pain. With no other options left, I compromised and began taking over the counter pain relievers, such as Tylenol, Excedrin, and Ibuprofen for the pain. While I'm still uncomfortable relying on these chemicals, they were the only things that relieved the pain long enough to let me function properly and complete my duties.

In April of 2011, a radio call flashed out about a robbery in progress for the Wells Fargo Bank at 17th and Walnut Streets. As a lieutenant, I always responded to all Part One crimes that occurred while I was on duty. These are the serious felonies, like homicides, robberies, burglaries, rapes, kidnappings and arsons. On my way to the robbery site, I travelled through the intersection of Broad and Walnut Streets... another vehicle plowed through the intersection and struck me. I had the right of way, but no one told the other car as they ran the red light and t-boned my cruiser. On the plus side, the vehicle that struck me was the getaway car for the robbery suspects.

I don't remember anything after the collision, since I suffered a concussion along with other injuries. I woke up in Hahnemann Hospital and had to get the details from the officers that were by my side. Apparently, the vehicle the suspects were driving was stolen. The suspects apparently survived unscathed and fled on foot from the stolen vehicle. After the collision, my vehicle was knocked into a traffic light pole, which totaled the front end. The entire left side of my patrol car was crushed in and I cracked my head on the computer in the vehicle.

While in the hospital, the doctor gave me the "good news" that I *only* suffered a concussion, fractured collarbone and a herniated disc in my back. I felt so much pain while I laid lifeless in the hospital for ten days. The only thing that kept my spirits up were the constant visits from my family and friends. I'll spare you the details, but the end result was an extensive back surgery and several physical therapy rehabilitation sessions afterwards.

Although I was injured while on duty, very little support came from the department. After being out of work for three months recovering, I was contacted by my captain regarding my future with the force. The department's only concern was whether they could place me on permanent disability or if I would be able to return to full duty. I felt that I had no other choice than to come back to work too soon, when I knew I wasn't physically at a hundred percent. I was only out of work for three months before the worker's compensation doctor claimed I was ready to go back, even though I expressed my concerns about the reoccurring pain in my back.

A week passed and I received a copy of a letter from the doctor via mail. The letter informed the department that I should have no issues coming back to full duty and would be able to return to work immediately. I was furious and could not believe this was happening to me. I tried everything from contacting the Fraternal Order of Police Union to writing a letter to the police commissioner, but no one would listen to me.

After battling with the department for over a month, I gave up and returned to work. I still didn't believe I was at a hundred percent, but I was ready to give as much as I could. I felt that I had no other choice if I was to maintain my position in the department. On my first day of returning to work, my back immediately began aching, barely two hours into my shift. I took some Ibuprofen, but it didn't completely relieve the pain. Throughout the rest of the week, the pain grew more constant and the medications I used for my previous back pain no longer relieved the new pain I suffered.

I contacted my personal doctor, along with the worker's compensation doctor, and informed them both that the medication was not working. I never heard back from the worker's compensation doctor. My personal doctor prescribed me a stronger pain medication called Percocet. During the first month of taking Percocet, all my pain was gone and I had no issues at work. Later, the medication began to have only a slight effect on my pain, which led to me taking twice the recommended dosage. Taking double the dosage was the only thing that worked and allowed me to function normally.

The only issue I ran into was finishing my prescribed quantity too fast, so I had to explain to my doctor what I was doing and why I needed refills so often. The doctor initially gave me the refills, but informed me he would not make a habit of doing so, because he feared my body would become dependent on the Percocet.

The next day, I attempted to work without taking the medication, but the excruciating pain in my back returned. I fought through the pain during work, but I could do nothing but sit at my desk all day. My sergeants and officers noticed a change in my work procedures because I was very active on the streets prior to getting injured. Whenever anyone expressed any concern for my wellbeing, I denied anything was wrong because I didn't want anyone looking into my situation or throwing me a pity party. When I got home from work, I could do nothing but lay in bed or on the couch because my back was throbbing incessantly. I could not sleep because the pain was too much to bear, so I had no other choice but to start taking the Percocets again. Knowing I wasn't supposed to, I took double the dosage since I knew it would give me immediate relief. Over the next year, I would take the Percocet with over-the-counter pain medications to avoid suspicion from my doctor. This worked for a while and I went back to being an active lieutenant.

In the spring of 2013, my district received information of burglaries and robberies occurring at local pharmacies throughout the city. During one night shift, I responded to a burglary at a CVS store at 18th and Chestnut Streets. Our initial investigation revealed that the suspects were chased by officers on foot and they ditched book bags that were filled with the stolen goods. I assisted with the search for the suspects. While driving in the area, I found a green book bag laying in the corner of an entrance to a parking garage. I knew this had to be one of the bags dropped by the suspects, so I picked it up. Upon opening the bag, I found it filled with gift cards, electronics and prescription pill bottles from the pharmacy. The prescription pill bottles were labeled "Hydrocodone" and "OxyContin."

I was approached by one of the investigating officers who stated, "Hello ma'am, we have two of the suspects in custody, but one got away."

"I think I found one of their bags. It has a bunch of stolen crap inside."

I overheard the officer transmit over the radio, "Dispatch, we have stolen gift cards and electronics, recovered from a bag dropped by the suspects. Notify the detectives that I'm in the area of 18th and Sansom Streets."

As he waited for the detectives to arrive on scene, I drove back to the district. There was an uneasy feeling of guilt in the back of my mind. When I got to the district, I went straight to the locker room and put the Hydrocodone and OxyContin in my purse. I sat down and wondered what forced me to do this. I had so many thoughts running through my head. What if someone discovered I took it? How am I going to get away with this? What if the CVS inventory comes back and they realize the pills had been taken? What if one of the suspects admits to taking the pills? What will my family think when they see the pills in the house? I immediately opened my locker, took the pills out of my purse and buried them in my locker under some equipment and clothing. My plan was to somehow return the pills to the investigating officer to place it into the evidence inventory. I just had to figure out how I would return them without making myself look suspicious.

Months went by and no mention ever came of the missing pills from the book bag. The third suspect from the burglary was never caught so there were still stolen items that were never recovered. That was good for me because everyone thought the pills were with the third suspect. I could not believe I actually got away with this. I always lived an honest life and had a stand-up career, but I was concerned that my career would collapse if I could not work because of my back problems. The guilt of stealing evidence haunted me for months. I continued to go back and forth about throwing the pills away or admitting I had taken them. I was on the verge of coming cleaning to my supervisor in August of 2013, but I had a major setback. The pain in my back was growing more frequent and I finished my prescribed medication sixteen days earlier than my next scheduled doctor's appointment. I tried to refill the prescription early, but it was declined by my doctor. I believe the date was around the 11th of August when I woke up in so much pain that I could not get out of bed. I had to call out from work and stayed in bed the entire day. I remember calling my doctor and the pharmacy over fifteen times, trying to get my pain medication refilled. After no success with my doctor, I tried taking several over-the-counter pain medications, but I needed something stronger. I didn't eat or sleep that entire day or night, because my only concern was my back.

The next day, I managed the pain with over-the-counter medications, just enough to get to work. Once I got to the district, I went straight to my locker and took three Hydrocodone pills. Within thirty minutes, my back pain went away and I was more than relieved. I was back to my normal self and performing my duties. The guilt I originally felt about taking the pills no longer haunted me, because I felt that I really needed them. Over the next few months, I managed the pain and was able to stock up on the Percocet that was prescribed from my doctor. I finished the Hydrocodone and was back taking my Percocets, and occasionally a few OxyContin pills. The OxyContin gave me so much pain relief, but I was always cautious because of its addictive characteristics. Everything was going well for me, until a visit with my doctor in January of 2014.

We talked about my back issue and he felt that I made a lot of progress, seeing as though I was not contacting him for refills of my medication constantly. He decided he wanted to lower my dosage of Percocet to slowly take me off the medication. I snapped in the doctor's office. I told him not to lower my dosage because he would ruin my life and my career. My little performance in the office didn't help the situation and my next script for the Percocet was for a lower dosage. I went from having 7.5mg pills to 2.5mg. This forced me to take three or four pills at a time rather than my usual two. It also forced me to take the OxyContin pills more often than I did before. The addiction to the pain medications slowly took over my body and without the medications, it seemed like I could not function normally. The only problem was the growing dependency my body developed for the pills. I went from taking one OxyContin when I felt pain to waking up every morning and starting my day off with a pill to avoid the pain. Slowly the one OxyContin turned into an OxyContin with a Percocet and continued to increase until I was taking both pills four times daily, in combination with other over-the-counter pain relievers. By January of 2014, I was out of the OxyContin pills and was left with just the Percocet. I was a complete mess. I wouldn't do much when I was home, except lay around and complain about no one wanting to help me. My behavior began affecting my marriage and relationship with my children. The only place I was able to keep it together was at work, because I knew I had to. With each passing day, I felt the pain in my back slowly creep up on me. I knew the only way to relieve the pain would be to find more OxyContin pills. That was the beginning of the downward spiral of my life.

With the position of lieutenant I held in the department, I was able to have unlimited access to the evidence locker and I had the opportunity to view all evidence before it was inventoried. Over the next few weeks, I made it my duty to check all evidence that came in from drug arrests. I was able to skim off several pills while reviewing evidence from specific drug cases. I would take three or four pills for every fifteen to thirty that came in to our possession. I did this for weeks until the district received criminal intelligence memorandums on a high profile drug dealer that the Narcotics Unit was watching in our area. I contacted the supervisor of the Narcotics Unit and offered assistance with manpower, by lending them some of my officers to assist with the investigation.

One Friday afternoon, the Narcotics Strike Force served a warrant on the drug dealer's home. Once inside, the suspect was arrested and tons of evidence was recovered from inside the home. Included in the evidence were OxyContin pills. While inside the home, officers began searching for other suspects and evidence. I knew if I didn't get everyone out of the home, I would not have an opportunity to grab the pills. I was the highest-ranking officer on the scene at that time, which meant I was in charge of the scene. I ordered everyone out of the home and claimed I would contact our detectives to come to the scene and photograph the evidence before it was inventoried. Once everyone exited the home, I was able to steal approximately 100 OxyContin pills. I stuffed the pills in my pockets, and even swallowed a few to ensure I would not feel any back pain anytime soon. I exited the home while I was on the phone with the detectives, which made everything seem normal and no one suspected anything. Detectives arrived on scene and inventoried the evidence, which included the remaining OxyContin pills, ecstasy pills, cocaine, several firearms and over $10,000 in cash.

Stealing the pills was very easy, but maintaining a low profile was very difficult. I was essentially always high on pills, which forced me to not be as active as I once was. I attempted to study to become a captain, but ended up failing because my focus was only on how I was going to get more pills. One evening I went out drinking with a few coworkers. My addiction was so serious, that I would forget how many pills I took because it became a normal routine for me. When I got to the bar, I began drinking several alcoholic beverages without realizing I had the medication in my system. It was March of 2014, and I ended up crashing my car into a tree when I left the bar. I suffered no injuries during that particular crash, but the responding officers suspected I was driving under the influence.

One of the officers asked, “Hello ma’am, have you been drinking tonight?”

I looked at the officer who appeared to be fresh out of the police academy and replied, “Do you know who I am? I’m a lieutenant and you have no right to speak to me like this.”

The officer appeared surprised and hesitated with his next response. “I apologize Lieutenant. I didn’t mean to offend you. I’m just doing my job.”

“You won’t have a job to do, if you continue to disrespect me.”

The officer immediately apologized a second time and offered to give me a ride home. I knew I used my authority to get over on those two, but I could care less. I demanded they leave the scene immediately. I ended up calling my husband to pick me up and told him we would need a tow-truck to take my vehicle.

During the ride home, my husband began questioning my recent behavior.

"Baby is everything ok with you? Things have been weird lately."

I thought about telling him the truth about everything, but I knew he would not understand what I was going through.

"Nothing's going on. I just had a rough day at work."

He stopped the car and just looked over at me for a moment. I was so drunk I couldn't focus, so I didn't look over at him. I knew he was frustrated that I wasn't responding, so he just drove home. My head began spinning and everything appeared to be blurry. I don't recall what happened after that, I just remember waking up the next day in our bed. I felt the urge to take some pills, but realized I was not currently in pain. I was so confused because I felt as if I could not move without taking a pill first. So what was once an urge to get rid of the pain, became an urge to properly function. My body felt weak and fatigued when I wasn't on the medication. At that moment, my husband came into the room and sat on the edge of the bed.

He handed me a pamphlet for a drug rehabilitation facility and said, "Baby, you need help."

"Are you fucking serious? Are you trying to call me a druggy? Get the fuck out, now!"

"I've seen the empty pill bottles, Sandra. I'm trying to help you. I'm trying to be supportive."

"I don't need your fucking help because I don't have a problem!"

As I yelled, our children began running in the room pleading for us to stop arguing. I could not deal with my husband at that time, so I gathered my belongings and took his car to work.

During the drive, I cried so hard because I knew something was wrong with me. Seeing the sad looks on my children's faces was heart breaking. I knew I needed help, but at that time I was in so much denial and didn't know how to deal with the problem. I considered taking a personal leave of absence from work, but I didn't want to lose everything I worked so hard for. I could not think of a good excuse to tell my captain, especially since news spread fast around the department. I intended on talking to my captain about taking leave once I got to the district, but I arrived just as some officers were bringing in a prisoner. It was a small time drug dealer who they arrested after serving a search warrant. When I walked into the district, I saw evidence from the arrest sitting on the table waiting to be processed. The evidence included OxyContin pills, among other drugs. As soon as I saw the pills, I felt the cravings coming along stronger than ever. I totally forgot my original intentions and my only concern was getting the pills. I attempted to get close to the evidence, but was unable to because the officers immediately began processing it. I waited around in my office, contemplating how I was going to get the pills.

I approached one of the officers and asked, "So what did you get here?"

"We've been watching this guy for months, Lieutenant, and we finally got him. He sells pills down 58th and Walnut," the officer replied.

"What did he have on him?"

"Some Zannies, Ecstasy and a bunch of Oxys."

I watched as he processed the drugs and placed them in the evidence room. I returned to my office to develop some type of plan, but time was not on my side. While in the office, so many ideas were going through my head. I wanted to go home, but my body wouldn't let me. It felt like someone stabbed me in the back and I really needed to get rid of the pain.

I walked towards the evidence room and saw the officer who was in charge of logging all evidence. I wanted him out of the way, so I ordered him to give me access to the evidence room. I went into the evidence bag that was recently processed and took thirty OxyContin pills. I placed the pills in my pocket and walked out the Evidence Room, like everything was normal. By the look on the officer's face, he didn't suspect a thing. I returned to my desk, took two of the pills and placed the rest in my purse. My pain temporarily went away, but I could not describe the satisfaction I received from just taking the pills. I sat back at my desk and enjoyed that brief feeling of satisfaction, which was quickly interrupted. Ironically, the captain walked passed and saw me.

"What are you doing here?"

"Um, I'm just catching up on some paperwork sir."

"So you're just here doing some paperwork, huh?" he asked, with a doubtful expression on his face.

"Yes," I nervously replied.

"Well what were you just doing in the evidence room?"

I began stuttering during my reply. "I – I – I was just making sure everything in there was in order, Captain. That's all I was doing."

He gave me a disbelieving stare, before walking away. At that moment, I was very nervous and didn't know if he realized what I had done. I decided to just leave before he built more suspicion and began looking into why I was really there. As I was walking out, I glanced over towards the Evidence Room and saw the captain talking to the Evidence Officer. I wondered what the captain was up to, but I didn't plan on sticking around to find out. I was walking towards the front door, when I heard the captain yell, "Lieutenant, wait a minute!"

I looked back and observed him walking towards me. I had to get out of the building before the captain could question me regarding any new information he had just received. Since my head was turned the wrong way, I ended up colliding into an officer that was walking in the front door. I guess I was too focused on the captain, to pay attention to who or what was actually in front of me. When we bumped into each other, my purse fell out of my hand and to the ground. Once my purse hit the ground, everything inside spilled out. It seemed like everything was in slow motion. All I could see were the pills I had just taken, rolling all over the floor. I became so nervous and it seemed like all eyes were on me at that moment. I dove on the ground trying to gather all the pills, but that seemed impossible. Everyone began helping me pick things up, including the captain who handed me my purse.

After the captain handed me my purse, he asked, "Is there anything I should know, Lieutenant?"

"No there isn't, sir. I just dropped my stuff."

"Ok, no problem. I'm going to let you go since you seem to be in such a hurry, but there are some things we need to discuss at a later time."

I knew he could see the fear in my eyes as I backed out the door.

After walking out the district, I sat in the car for an hour. I intended on going straight home, but I was frozen in suspense. What did the captain want to talk about? What was he doing at the Evidence Room? Did he see me take the pills? I had so many unanswered questions in my head and they were driving me crazy. I began organizing my purse to make sure I didn't leave anything behind. After counting the pills, I slammed my head on the steering wheel because I was missing one. I only had twenty-seven of the twenty-eight pills I had taken. I started sweating profusely and panicking. I felt an uncontrollable urge take over my body and I was determined to find that other pill. My emotions got the best of me and I began craving the medication. My mouth began to water and I began feeling warm. I immediately swallowed one of the pills to relax myself during that stressful moment, but I still had to solve my current problem. I needed to go back in the building to find the other pill, so I made the decision to do so. I quickly walked backed into the district and as I did, a tall figure stood in the doorway. It was the captain and he appeared to be waiting for my return.

He looked at me and asked, “Did you forget something, Lieutenant?”

I couldn’t even focus enough to answer him. My eyes looked pass him and scanned the floor for the pill. I zoned out and didn’t respond to him at all.

Suddenly I heard a loud bolstering voice yell, “I asked you a question, Lieutenant. What are you looking for and why are you back here?”

“Um, I came back to use the bathroom.”

At that moment, I grew angry and yelled myself. “With all due respect sir, you keep questioning me like I’m a criminal or something. This is beginning to feel like harassment.”

“Harassment? Are you serious? That’s the route you want to take with me?”

He slammed his fist against the door and yelled, “You show up to my district when you’re not supposed to be here and you go snooping around in my Evidence Room. You leave the building and come right back in looking for something. You are definitely up to something and I’m going to find out exactly what it is.”

The captain stomped away and went into his office, slamming the door behind him. I could care less about his little suspicion, this was my opportunity to find the pill and I immediately began looking on the floor for it. Officers began walking by and asking if I was ok. I'm sure it had to be a little odd to see your lieutenant on her hands and knees looking for something that obviously wasn't there. I ignored everyone and continued my search. I could hear the whispers of people walking by calling me "crazy" and "weird." After searching and being unable to locate the pill, my hands and clothes were filthy. I stood up and staggered out of the building, back towards the car. When I got to the car, I felt nauseous and vomited over the rear bumper. I felt so weak for some reason, so I slowly eased myself inside the car and dosed off.

Time passed as I slept in the car. My shift was supposed to begin at 4:00 pm and it was now 9:30 pm.

I was startled by the sound of someone banging on the car window, followed up by a concerned voice yelling, "Sandra, wake up! Sandra, get up! Get up honey!"

When I looked up, I saw my husband standing outside the vehicle. I rolled down the window and he asked, "Honey what is going on. Are you ok?"

"What the hell are you doing here?"

"Your captain called and wanted to speak to me about you. I think he's concerned because you have been acting a little strange lately."

I jumped up out my seat and pushed my husband.

"What do you mean the captain called you? When did he call? What did you tell him?"

"He called me at 4:30 pm because you never showed up to work. We didn't know where you were. Why are you parked out here sleeping and not inside working? The captain said he was concerned that something was wrong with you today. What were you doing up here before your shift? You just stormed out the house and didn't say a word to me or the kids. I thought something bad happened to you."

I pushed him again and marched into the captain's office. When I walked in, he was talking to the detective supervisors. I walked right by them and got into the captain's face.

"What the hell do you think you're doing? I told you to stop harassing me and you decided to call my husband."

The captain backed up and stated, "You need to stand down, Lieutenant. You march into my office and disrespect me in front of your peers. You have vomit and dirt all over you. You look a mess. You need to leave my office immediately."

"No, I will not leave because you owe me an explanation. Why are you calling my husband up here?"

He smirked. "I simply called him because I found an OxyContin pill on the ground and couldn't get in touch with you to ask if it was yours. It's ok, because when I called him, he let me know you don't have a prescription for this pill. That is very interesting."

I looked at the captain and knew at that moment that I couldn't admit the pill was mine.

"I don't know what you're talking about. That can't be my pill. Since you're doing a personal investigation, I suggest you figure out who the pill really belongs to."

I looked around the room and I could tell everyone was in shock by the way I was speaking to the captain. He appeared to be very angry with me, as I watched his pale face turn bright red.

He stared me down. "Lieutenant, how dare you speak to me in such a fashion? Mr. Smith, I suggest you take your wife home before she gets herself in a lot of trouble."

My husband held my hand and whispered, "Honey, let's go home."

I realized at that moment it was in my best interest to just leave. We walked outside and my head began to throb. A strong headache came over me and I began craving the OxyContin. The urges became very uncontrollable. I was very angry with my husband, but I didn't have the energy to argue with him. I told him not to say a word to me for the rest of the night. When I got in the car, the first thing I did was take a pill. My husband looked over at me and just shook his head. As we drove off, I could see officers from the district staring at me. I could only imagine what they were thinking, after hearing all the screaming and yelling the captain and I did.

When we got home, I walked inside to the sight of my children all sitting in the living room. It seemed as if they were all waiting for me to return home. The room appeared to be set up for some type of intervention. Once I recognized what was going on, I immediately walked into my bedroom. The kids came up and attempted to plead with me about finding out what was going on in my life. I briefly remember the night because I locked myself in the bathroom to get away from them. I sat on the toilet and cried my eyes out. I was so stressed and was not in the mood to deal with anyone. I had not eaten all day and I felt sick to my stomach. The last thing I remember from that night was taking two more pills and laying down on the bathroom floor. When I woke up, I was in the hospital with all types of tubes running through my body. It was a complete shock because I had no idea why I was in the hospital or how I got there. I looked over and saw my husband and children sitting by my side.

The doctor walked into the room and stated, "Oh hello, Mrs. Smith. I see you're finally awake. Do you know what happened?"

I nodded my head no and he went on to explain what led up to my trip to the hospital.

"Well, you are here because you tried to hurt yourself. Apparently, you overdosed on pills while you were in your bathroom. Your husband found some medication near you, which we believe are OxyContin."

I sat up and asked, "Where are my pills?"

"Those pills were confiscated because it does not appear that you have a prescription for them."

I turned my head away from him and began crying.

He noticed I was upset. "Mrs. Smith, everything is going to be ok. The only thing I need you to do now is get some rest. If you need anything, just press that red button next to your bed and a nurse will come right in. I will be back to check on you in about an hour or so."

I could not believe what was going on. I blamed my husband for everything. There was no reason he should have been talking to my captain and he shouldn't have let the kids try to set me up with an intervention. My main concern was getting out of the hospital and going to work, but my children let me know the doctor planned on keeping me overnight for observations. I had my husband call my captain to let him know I would not be going to work. I'm pretty sure the captain wanted to know my reasoning, but I made sure my husband told him I just had a simple cold. My hospital stay was not bad at all. I finally had time to relax, so I had nothing to complain about. The nurses seemed very concerned about my well-being and they made sure I ate and stayed hydrated. My family was by my side the entire time. I had slight drug cravings during my stay, but they were not intense and usually went away within an hour. I was given some medication for my occasional back pain, but it was in very low dosages. Everything went well during my brief stay and I was released from the hospital the next night.

The night I left, I went home with my family and we sat down to talk. They were advised by the doctor to discuss my need to over-medicate myself. They really wanted me to consider attending a rehabilitation facility, just for a tour, so I could get a better idea of what the facility offered. I attempted to convince them my problem could only be resolved with medication and physical therapy, but they didn't seem to agree. This frustrated me and I shut down. I began to feel a craving coming along, which made me lose focus on the conversations that were taking place. I told everyone I wanted to rest for the night and used that opportunity to check my purse for the OxyContin pills. I was sure that they left a few behind somewhere, but I was sadly mistaken.

What started as me looking through my purse, eventually led to me tearing the room apart. I became more paranoid and fatigued as time passed. I attempted to fight the urge, but it was not working. I stayed up all night long, while my back throbbed. I was so restless and never got any sleep that night. I locked my husband out of the room because I didn't want him to see the mess and get concerned. By the next morning, I was curled up in a fetal position on the floor.

I was in excruciating pain, so I decided to take my usual combination of over-the-counter pain medications. Although I still felt a slight throbbing pain in my back, I was able to manage. Throughout the day I contemplated taking more medication, but I was reluctant from doing so because of my little hospital visit. I decided to rest all day because I was scheduled to work that evening. I chose to go into work a little early, so I left about two hours prior to my shift. I lived in the Roxborough section of Philadelphia and driving downtown to the district meant I had to travel through some of the rougher neighborhoods in the city. While driving to work, I was having very bad cravings again. Some of the neighborhoods I drove through were known drug areas and I decided to stop at one to inquire about some pills. This place was 10th Street and Montgomery Avenue. When I drove through the neighborhood, I saw a group of young men standing on the corner and I figured they had to be selling something. I pulled up to the group and one of them walked over to the car.

"What's up lady, you lost?"

"No, I'm not lost. I'm looking for something."

"Oh really, what you looking for?"

"Some pills" I stated, "OxyContin."

He looked around and laughed. "Oh ok, so you want some Oxys?"

"Yes, please."

"So what makes you think that we have any?"

"I don't know if you do, that's why I stopped to ask."

"Where you from? I never saw you around here before."

"I'm not from this area. I usually get what I need from someone else."

"Well this is how it's going to go down. You pay me and I'll call my old head and let him know what you want. Then you'll drive up to 12th Street to pick them up."

"Ok. That works for me."

I gave him a hundred and fifty dollars and he said, "Ok. I'll tell him you're on the way. His name is Cash."

"What does he look like?"

"You'll see when you meet him," he said and laughed.

He walked back towards his group and I drove up to 12th Street and waited for "Cash." I looked around and saw many people out, but no one approached the car. About twenty minutes passed and I was still just sitting there. I had a very bad feeling about being in that neighborhood, but I had to get some pills. Finally, I saw a guy walking towards my direction. I still remember exactly what he looked like. He was a black male with dark skin. He had a full beard and a dollar sign tattoo under his right eye. He was wearing a black hoodie that had some type of weird design printed on the back. The closer he got to the car, the more my heart rate sped up. He knocked on my window and I reluctantly rolled it down. I was so nervous when he looked at me.

In his very deep voice, he asked, "Oxys?"

I looked straight and nodded my head. He stared me down for almost a minute and then began looking around. Suddenly he pulled a gun out from his waistband and put it to the left side of my head. I was so scared and didn't know what to do. I didn't know if he was going to shoot me, rob me or worse. My badge was in my purse and I didn't want him to notice it, if he robbed me. I never carried my gun off duty, so I had no way of defending myself.

I began crying and he said, "Listen bitch, I don't know if you're fucking stupid or you got a death wish, but you need to get the fuck out of here."

"I just came here for some pills, please don't hurt me." My whole life flashed before my eyes, as I felt the cold steel on my temple.

"Well you ain't getting no pills from here bitch. You got five second to bull off before I blow you're fucking brains out."

I immediately sped off and didn't stop until I got far away from that neighborhood. I thought about calling up the local district and have them haul "Cash" in for pulling a gun on me, but I would not be able to justify why I was in that neighborhood. I was literally powerless and I couldn't believe what just happened to me. That was a very stupid decision and I was lucky he didn't do more than just threaten me. That brief brush with death made me forget about my back pain for a while.

I walked into the district and the first person I saw was the captain. He looked like he saw a ghost when I walked in the building. He immediately went into his office and closed the door. I paid him no mind and sat at my desk, as my cravings got worse. My sergeant and other officers approached me with greetings and I tried my best to entertain them, but they could see the agony on my face. From my desk, I could see the captain walking around, which was odd because he usually leaves unless there is a big job or he needed to speak to someone on the evening or night shift. I ignored him and not once approached him to discuss my brief absence. My back began throbbing and the only thing I could think of doing was to go into the Evidence Room to search for more pills. I walked over to the Evidence Room, but an officer was posted there and I knew there would be no way to distract him long enough to search for some pills. From a distance, I could hear a commotion in the intake area. Some officers had brought in a prisoner and I had to see what was going on. As soon as I walked in the intake area, I saw one of the officers bring in an evidence bag that was filled with prescription pill bottles. The captain walked right out and asked them what they had.

One of the officers replied, "We got a drug bust. This dude was out there trying to sell pills in Reading Terminal."

"Good work," the captain nodded and left the building.

My mouth began to water as I gazed at the pill bottles. I walked back to my desk, wondering what kind of pills were in the bag. My cravings grew ever more intense and I had no means of satisfying them. Suddenly the commotion in the intake area quieted and the officers took the suspect into the processing area. I walked into the intake area and saw the evidence bag still sitting on the table, with nobody around. I couldn't help but wonder what was inside the bag, so I immediately looked into the bag and went through the bottles. Among all the bottles, I found two that were labeled OxyContin and contained thirty pills each. Jackpot, that was just what I needed. I quickly opened both bottles and took ten pills from each bottle. I closed the bag and went back to my desk. As soon as I sat down, I wasted no time before taking two pills. The rest of the pills were placed into my purse. I was in a very good space once the pills were in my system. After about two hours, the captain walked back into the building and approached me. I gave him a very sinister glare as he stood in front of me. He told me he needed to talk to me in his office. I had no idea what he needed to talk about, but I figured it was about my absences during the time of my overdose.

Upon walking into the office, I observed four people already standing around his desk. My mouth dropped and I was immediately in shock. Out of the four people standing in the office, two of them were the officers I observed with the arrest and one was their suspect. The fourth person was well dressed in a suit and was holding the evidence bag that was previously in the intake area.

The captain closed the door. "Lieutenant Smith, I'd like to introduce you to Detective Williams, Lieutenant

Jones, Lieutenant Mercado and Captain Barnes from Internal Affairs. They are here conducting an investigation on you, with the concern that you have been stealing drugs evidence."

I became very emotional and began crying because I knew I was in a lot of trouble.

Captain Barnes stepped up and asked, "Lieutenant, we watched you when you took the pills out of this bag. What did you do with them?"

"Most of them are in my purse at my desk."

"Most of them?"

"Yes, I took two because I needed them for my back. The rest are in my purse. I'm so sorry."

"Ok Lieutenant, I know this is going to be hard for you and we are going to allow you time to obtain legal representation, because you're going to need it. We know this is not the first time you took some pills and we got a call from some undercover narcotics officers that followed you from a known drug area to the district earlier this evening. Just so you know, you could have gotten yourself killed today. They arrested a gangbanger named "Cash" that apparently pulled a gun out on you."

"Yes, he did."

"Well you will be needed to testify against him, when the time comes."

My captain just shook his head as he heard this. He obviously knew nothing about it at all. I felt so weak. I just wanted to pass out right where I stood.

"So what do I do now?"

My captain just looked at me. "You contact an attorney. You're going to be facing criminal charges."

Once he said criminal charges, I broke down.

Captain Barnes looked at me and said, "Like I told you before, we are going to give you the opportunity to go home to your family and contact a lawyer. You need to report to the Internal Affairs Headquarters by 2:00 pm tomorrow. You can call someone to come pick you up, since we still have work to do."

The captain allowed me to sit in his office and call my husband. While on the phone with my husband, I observed one of the detectives taking photographs of my desk and purse. After doing that, he walked outside to photograph the vehicle I was driving. I could not believe I was so stupid to fall for their trap. I was pissed at my captain because I knew he had to be the one to set me up. At that time, I could do nothing but wonder what my next move was going to be. I just simply wanted to die right then and there. All my years of hard work just went right out the window. My life was ruined.

After about an hour, my husband finally arrived at the district. I gave Captain Barnes the pills from my purse and they allowed me to leave. I was in total disbelief of what just took place. I could not believe what was going on. My husband didn't say one word to me on the way home or when we arrived. I could do nothing that night except cry myself to sleep. Upon waking up the next morning, my husband had already contacted my union representative and a criminal lawyer. I came downstairs and saw him sitting in the kitchen. I walked right over and gave him the biggest hug in the world.

I whispered in his ear, "I need help."

He looked at me and quietly said, "You are going to get the help you need, honey."

Time flew by that day and before I knew, it was 1:00 pm. We headed out to go to the Internal Affairs building. It was another silent ride. My back began throbbing, but I fought through the pain because my mind was elsewhere. We arrived at our destination and were met by the attorneys and Captain Barnes. Captain

Barnes asked me to make a formal statement regarding everything I was accused of. I felt so many emotions and was still in shock. I was instructed by the attorneys to remain silent and was immediately placed under arrest. As they walked me back towards their processing area, I looked back towards my husband, who was on his knees in tears. At that moment, seeing him so hurt, I knew what pain really was. No drug in the world could relieve it.

Lieutenant Sandra Smith was charged and found guilty of theft and related offenses. She served one year in jail and was released on parole. She was terminated from the Philadelphia Police Department. She is currently seeking help in a drug rehabilitation facility in Florida.

CHAPTER TWO

As a former serviceman and ten-year veteran of the Philadelphia Police Department, protecting the innocent was rooted deep in Officer Hoover Townsend's DNA. He grew up in the West Philadelphia area of the city and witnessed countless acts of abuse as a child. His father was physically abusive towards his mother, which led to their divorce when Hoover was in his early teens. At first glance, Hoover came through the ordeal well-adjusted and eventually joined the United States Army as a young man. After finishing his tour of duty, he signed up for the police academy and found a new way to help the helpless as a Philadelphia police officer. Officer Townsend went on to have a very productive career in the 19th District, which covered parts of West Philadelphia. He was especially known for his sympathy and compassion with handling domestic violence incidents, after witnessing what his mother had to deal with for years. Unfortunately, his passion soon turned to obsession and led him down a dark road one winter night in October of 2010.

This is Officer Hoover Townsend's story...

DOMESTIC VIOLENCE

I worked the overnight (12:00 am to 8:00 am) shift at the 19th District. My normal routine was to arrive at work early and workout before roll call, which started at 12:00 sharp. I worked with Officer Anthony Colon, who was a great guy. He used to be a boxer and had no problem throwing hands with all the "tough guys" in the hood. We used to get in some good workouts that helped prepare us for the physicality of the job. We were very active officers and had been through a lot of dangerous situations together. Colon knew my stance on domestic violence and knew I took it very serious. Every domestic call we handled was personal to me. After seeing what my mom went through, I was skeptical about the way the justice system handled domestics. Their answer to every situation was issuing Protection from Abuse orders, which rarely worked. Those orders were violated on a daily basis. In most of our serious domestic violence cases, we always discovered the suspects had valid PFA orders against them. Although those orders were constantly violated, no one did anything about it. No one truly cared about the victims and what they had to suffer when they discovered the courts were not really protecting them.

Throughout my ten-year career, nothing compared to what happened in 2010. One night, I received a phone call right after roll call ended. The call was from my nineteen-year-old cousin, Tiffany.

As soon as I answered her call, I could hear Tiffany screaming into the phone. "He hit me! I need help."

Tiffany lived with her 28-year-old boyfriend in Southwest Philadelphia, and he was no good. Her boyfriend was a fake thug, who our family didn't like at all. Nine years was a big age difference and once our family expressed our dislike for her boyfriend, Tiffany shut down and kept a lot of things from us. We tried many times to tell Tiffany to leave him alone, but she never did. She was the typical young teen who thought she was madly in love and stuck by his side. She was so eager to act like an adult and be out of her parent's house, she settled for a control freak with an intense criminal background.

For every second I was on the phone listening to her screams, I became angrier. This situation was a clear reminder of my past. I couldn't waste any time getting to Tiffany, so I ran out the district door to head over and help her. I didn't tell my supervisor what my plans were, because I didn't want to be stopped.

As I was getting into the patrol vehicle, I heard, "Is everything ok, Hoov?" I looked up and saw Colon standing at the passenger side of the vehicle.

"Not at all, I think my little cousin's boyfriend attacked her tonight. She just called me and it didn't sound good."

After telling him the situation, he said, "Well come on and let's go over there." One thing I could certainly say is that Colon always had my back.

We drove over to Southwest Philly with the patrol car's lights and siren activated. I had to be driving over a hundred miles an hour to get there and was not concerned about anything but Tiffany's safety. The worst feeling in the world is not being able to help a loved one. I dealt with that guilt for years, back when my dad was abusing my mom every day. The only concern was that Tiffany and her boyfriend lived in the 12th District. We weren't necessarily allowed to be over there, so I knew this had to be quick. Officers had to have permission to go into another district, if they weren't on a specific assignment or detail. Obviously we had no permission to be anywhere near the 12th District, but I was willing to deal with the consequences if we got caught over there. The house was on the 5700 block of Florence Avenue. We pulled up on the curb and I ran up to the house.

He lived in a row home and the neighbors on both sides of his house were outside on their porches. There was no possible way they hadn't heard Tiffany's cries for help, but I knew it was common for people in Philly to turn the other cheek and not get involved in anything if it didn't directly affect them in some way. Especially when you lived next to a thug.

The front door was locked and I loudly banged on the door, hoping to get Tiffany's attention. There was no answer at the door and suddenly I heard screams coming from inside. I had to get in there immediately, so I began kicking the door. I pulled my right foot back and thrusted my leg forward with all my strength. After three strong kicks, the frame around the door broke and the door flew in. I ran into the home and everything was disheveled. It was obvious that a struggle had ensued inside the home. There were things thrown around the entire living room and a glass table was broken. I had to literally step over things to try and find out which room Tiffany was in. I heard screams coming from the kitchen and as I looked, I saw Tiffany's boyfriend choking her up against the wall.

I immediately ran towards the kitchen, drew my firearm and put it to the back of his head. My finger was on the trigger and my eyes followed the rear sights, which were perfectly aligned with the rear of his head. My hand was slightly shaking and sweat beads began to form on my forehead. I wanted to pull the trigger so bad, but I didn't want to award him the satisfaction of not dealing with the consequences of his actions. He attempted to turn back and look towards me, which forced me to reposition my firearm from the back of his head to his right temple.

Once I did this, he asked, "How the fuck did you get in my house?"

"Shut the fuck up, you piece of shit, before I blow your brains out."

"Oh, you must be the cop cousin. I don't know why you got your gun out. You ain't going to do shit with it, pig."

"You want to bet on that."

"Yea I do motherfucker. Go ahead and pull the trigger and end up all over the news dumbass."

"One more word from you and I will pull this trigger."

"Fuck you pig."

After hearing him say that, I hit him across the head with the butt of the firearm. He fell to the ground, which loosened his grip and freed Tiffany. As he fell to the ground, he reached up and attempted to grab my shirt. I continued striking him on the head and face. With each blow, I could see his face begin to swell up. My anger took over and I continued to reach back and strike him with great force. Blood was pouring from his head and he began losing consciousness. I shoved the barrel of my firearm down his throat and had every intention on pulling the trigger, but I felt a set of hands pulling me back. Out of my peripheral, I could see Colon pulling my shirt and Tiffany crying.

"That's enough! Enough!" Colon yelled. "He's not worth it."

He grabbed and pulled me outside. Tiffany also came running out behind us. I looked down and observed blood all over my uniform. I looked back up and saw the same neighbors standing out of the porch and they were looking right at me. I knew we had to leave the area because more neighbors began coming out of their homes trying to see what was going on.

"Is he dead?" Tiffany asked.

I looked at her face and saw all the bruises he put on her. "Don't worry about him. Go to the hospital and get checked out."

Tiffany ran to her car, which was parked in front of the house. She was fumbling with her keys, before eventually getting her car to start. Tiffany sped off and we followed right behind her. She headed towards the hospital, which was in West Philly. After she pulled into Mercy Hospital, Colon and I drove back to the district.

"What the hell am I going to do with this shirt?" I asked Colon.

"Get rid of it, ASAP. Do you have more shirts in your locker?"

"Yeah, should be a few in there."

"Well, I'll run in and get you a fresh one."

Once we got back to the district, I waited in the patrol car, as Colon went down to my locker to get me a clean shirt. My head was on a swivel the entire time, making sure no one walked by and saw my bloody uniform. Luckily, everyone was on patrol and the parking lot was clear. While I was sitting in the car, I was still in a state of shock. I really couldn't believe what just occurred and reality began kicking in. Many thoughts ran through my head. Will there be some sort of retaliation? Did someone call the police? Will he put his hands on my little cousin again? Was Tiffany even safe being at the hospital by herself? Colon came back out with a fresh shirt and pair of pants. We drove to an empty parking lot so I could change. After changing my uniform, I looked at my gun and it was covered with blood. I wiped off my firearm with the bloody shirt, put the shirt in a trash bag with the pants, and threw it in a dumpster behind one of the local corner stores. I looked at Colon and just shook my head.

"I'm sorry man, I just snapped."

"Listen, you don't have to explain anything to me. I would have done the same thing if some punk put his hands on someone in my family."

Throughout that night, I monitored the radio to see if a call was going to come out in the 12th District for the fight that occurred. Although I was worried about the possibility of someone calling the police, I truly believed he wouldn't do it because he would have to explain why I came to his home in the first place. He would literally have to admit he was hitting my cousin in order for him to justify any allegation against me. We made it through the whole shift and nothing ever came up.

After getting home, I tried to get some type of sleep but it was impossible. Every time I closed my eyes, I pictured what occurred earlier. It was like a scene from a movie replaying over and over in my head. I kept wondering what the final result would be and if I would need to handle him again. A part of me wanted to go back over to his house and tell him to fight me, but who knows who was at the house with him. I would have probably been walking into an ambush or something.

Time flew by and the night quickly turned to morning. I sat up all day staring at the ceiling and thinking about all the abuse my father put my mother through. Although I was a kid when it all happened, I should have tried to do more. I refused to stand by while any woman went through the same ordeal my mother had to go through. I went back and forth wondering if I should have just called the 12th District and have Tiffany's boyfriend arrested, but I knew the court systems would not properly address the situation. I knew they wouldn't be able to protect her, so I had to take it into my own hands. I ended up falling asleep for a couple of hours, when I was suddenly awakened by the constant ringing of my cell phone. I answered the phone and it was Colon checking on me.

"Are you good, bro? I couldn't sleep because I wanted to make sure you were cool."

"Yea I'm cool, just wondering what that mother fucker's next move is going to be."

"Man whatever move he makes won't mean shit. He better stay in his place."

"Yeah I know, but I still haven't heard from Tiffany."

"Well I'm sure she's ok. She might actually still be at the hospital and you know you get no cell phone service in the hospital."

"You're probably right. I just have to do something to take my mind off all this stuff."

"Let's go hit up the gym, so you can work off all that frustration."

I didn't regret my decision, but I definitely needed to do something to clear my head. I accepted Colon's offer and we ended up meeting at the gym for a quick workout after getting off the phone.

After our workout, I saw that I had several missed calls to my cell phone. The calls were from unknown numbers and there were no voicemails left. I had a gut feeling that the calls were related to the incident, but I wasn't too sure. I continued with my day and went to work that night. When I arrived at work, I received several noticeable stares from my fellow officers as if they knew what occurred last night. Once I saw that, I knew I had to be in some type of trouble. Upon walking into the roll call room, I observed three males that appeared to be detectives talking to my sergeant. I had a hunch they were there for me and was ready to deal with whatever form of discipline I was about to face. I looked behind the detectives and observed Colon standing in the corner with a worried look on his face.

The last thing he needed was to be dragged into my nonsense and I definitely didn't want him involved. One of the detectives walked over to me and introduced himself as Sergeant Domingo from the Internal Affairs Bureau. The only thing I knew about Internal Affairs was that they were cops whose job was to fire other cops. Since they were here for me, I guess that was the consequence of my actions.

"Do you know why we are here?" he asked.

"No sir, I have no idea why you are here."

"Well, I need to discuss an incident that occurred last night, involving Tiffany Townsend."

"What about Tiffany?"

"She's a relative of yours correct?"

"Yes she is, but what incident are you referring to, sir?"

"I'd prefer if we spoke in private."

I was taken into an interview room at our district to speak with Sergeant Domingo and the other guys from Internal Affairs. It was very awkward because I used that room numerous times to interview criminals and now I was sitting in the hot seat. I was so nervous because I didn't know what or how much they knew about the actual altercation. I tried to think of many ways to get myself out of what happened, but I didn't want to drag anyone else down with me and didn't want to make things worse for myself. Sergeant Domingo pulled out his phone and scrolled through three photographs of Tiffany's boyfriend. The photographs appeared to have been taken in the hospital and showed facial injuries that were stitched up. I could tell I did one hell of a job on his face. I was actually happy about this. Sergeant Domingo saw the smirk on my face and put his phone away.

"You will have the opportunity to tell us your side of the story soon," he said.

“What’s really going on?”

“We received a report today from one of this young man’s family members, informing us that he was assaulted by his girlfriend’s cousin, who’s a police officer. Luckily for you, we went over to the hospital to interview him and he told us he didn’t want to cooperate.”

‘Did he call you pigs?” I asked in a joking manner, but Sergeant Domingo didn’t seem to be too amused.

So many thoughts were running through my head and I contemplated telling them exactly what happened. By the looks on their faces, I knew they were not on my side. I had no idea what else to tell them.

“We think we have a pretty good idea of what happened. We just want to know if you are going to tell us the truth.”

I had nothing else to say to the sergeant. “Well, if we’re done here, I need to get back to work,” I said as I stood up and walked out. I honestly expected one of them to stop me from walking out, but they didn’t. Colon was waiting right outside the interview room. He came up to me all worried, but I told him everything was cool.

After roll call, I decided to call Tiffany to check up on her. As soon as I stepped out the building, I saw a car that I recognized driving by the district. It was a newer model, red Dodge Challenger with white racing stripes and huge chrome rims. At that moment, I remembered that Tiffany’s boyfriend had a similar car, because the crew he hangs around started a car club called “The Philly Dodge Squad.” Their crew all drove Dodge vehicles, mostly Chargers and Challengers that were all hooked up with rims and racing kits. I wasn’t sure if that was a coincidence or if it was someone her boyfriend sent over here. I continued looking and saw a white Charger driving slowly down the street. The driver of the Charger rolled his window down and gave me the middle finger. I couldn't really see who the driver was, so I began walking to the street to get a closer look. When I did, the red Challenger came back around and another one was driving right behind it.

They all drove around, circling the block and watching me. I figured this was meant to be some form of intimidation, but it didn't work. I called Colon outside so we could stop one of the cars. My focus was on the initial red Challenger. We quickly got into our patrol car and got behind the Challenger. Once we did so, it seemed like all the other cars drove away in different directions. The driver of the red Challenger realized we were behind him, so he turned on 59th Street and sped off. We turned on the lights and siren and attempted to conduct a traffic stop on the vehicle. My justification for the stop was going to be the fact the driver didn't use his turn signal when he made the turn onto 59th Street. The Challenger didn't stop for us and increased speed. He ended up losing control and crashing into a stop sign at the intersection of 59th and Arch Streets. When we reached the intersection, we drew our firearms and approached the car. There was only one guy in the car. His face was covered in tattoos and I knew he had to be a part of the crew that Tiffany's boyfriend belonged to.

I pointed my firearm at him and asked, "What's your name?"

He looked me up and down and replied, "My name is King Cutta. Get that fucking gun out my face."

"What kind of name is that?"

"Why the hell are you worried about it? I don't fuck with twelve, so get the fuck out of here." He began reaching for something in his car.

"Let me see your hands."

He lifted his hands up. I pulled him from the car and slammed him on the ground.

"Oh you going to beat me up too, huh?"

"What the hell is that supposed to mean?" I asked.

"I know who you are, bruh. You're Tiffany's cousin. The nut ass cop that beat up my boy Shizz Mack the other night," he said.

I was slightly in shock because I wasn't expecting him to say that. I placed him in handcuffs and put him in the back of the patrol car. Colon checked his Challenger, but there were no signs of drugs or weapons inside it.

I got in my patrol car and asked him, "What the hell are you doing? Why were you running from us?"

"I was running from you 'cause you like beating up on people for no reason."

"Oh, so you don't think putting your hands on a woman is a reason?"

"Man, fuck that bitch. If she acted like a woman, she would have got treated like one."

I hopped out the car, opened the back door and grabbed him around his neck.

"Who the fuck are you calling a bitch?"

I snapped and was ready to beat the shit out of him. All of a sudden, I heard a woman's voice yelling, "What are you doing? Get your hands off him."

I turned and saw several people walking towards our vehicle, recording me with their phones and cameras. This was typical, people always intervene and they don't know what's going on. Colon and I got back into the patrol car and drove the suspect to the district.

When we got back to the district, we processed the suspect under Fleeing and Eluding charges. Processing him was bitter and sweet. I was happy we got one of these dudes off the streets, but I never got the opportunity to find out why he was outside the district.

His real name was Khalif Thompson and he had an extensive criminal history. Which consisted of burglaries, robberies, firearms violations, aggravated assaults, and resisting arrest. A part of me wondered why he didn't put up much of a fight when we just arrested him. While we did an inventory of his belongings, I went through his phone to find "Shizz Mack's" phone number. After the processing was complete, I called the number from his phone and someone answered.

"Yo! What up?" he said.

"How's your face, punk?"

"Who the fuck is this?"

"You know exactly who this is. What was the point of you sending your boys around here?"

He immediately hung the phone up on me. I knew he wouldn't pick up if I called again, so I put the phone back with the suspect's belongings and went outside to get some fresh air. I called Tiffany to check on her, but she didn't answer. Colon walked out and put his hand on my shoulder.

"Is everything going to be ok?"

"I have no idea. There's no telling what these dudes are up to."

"I know and if they were outside the district, they will definitely be back."

"Well we need to be ready if they do come back here."

Just as I said that, two black Challengers rode slowly down the street and stopped directly in front the district. I couldn't see inside the cars because the windows were heavily tinted. I began running towards the cars and they both sped off. Colon had a serious look of concern on his face, but he didn't say a word. Throughout the rest of the night, things were pretty quiet. There were no more signs of anyone else from

Shizz Mack's crew, but I still wasn't going to put my guard down. My only concern was the fact that Tiffany had not contacted me back yet. I figured she had to be asleep, so I just waited patiently and decided I would call her back later.

That morning we got off work seemed like any other. Colon and I didn't discuss the Shizz Mack incident any further and it was off my mind for a while. I was driving home on I-76, like I always do, and I observed a vehicle that appeared to be following me. Every time I changed a lane, so did the vehicle behind me. Initially I didn't think much of it, so I got off at the next exit and pulled over. The vehicle passed me and I saw it was a blue Dodge Charger. I knew it had to be one of Shizz Mack's boys, so I began following him. He pulled up to a red light at Wayne Avenue and I stopped right behind him.

I pulled out my gun, hopped out the car and approached his. I yanked his door handle in an attempt to open it, but he sped off through the red light. I got into my vehicle and tried to follow him, but traffic was flowing and I had to wait for the light to change. By the time the light changed, I no longer had a visual on the Charger. I searched the whole area and couldn't find it. I had no idea where the Charger went that fast, but I grew more concerned about Tiffany because they could be doing the same thing to her. I called her phone again and she didn't answer. I drove home to check to see if any of those punks went to my house. It didn't appear that they knew where I lived, so that gave me some slight relief. My main concern at that time was still Tiffany. I had no idea who she could be staying with, since she left her boyfriend. I decided to go to her mother's house in West Philly. I drove up to the house and my Aunt Kim answered the door.

"Get in here quick," she whispered, as she pulled me inside the house.

"What's going on, Aunt Kim?"

She looked paranoid and was peeking out the front window. "I don't want them to see you."

"You don't want who to see me?"

"Those boys that hang with Tiffany's boyfriend. They have been riding up and down the block since last night. Three of them actually knocked on the door last night and asked for Tiffany."

"Where is Tiffany at now? Is she ok?"

"Yes, she's ok. She's upstairs."

I immediately went upstairs and saw Tiffany in the back room crying.

"Tiff, you had me worried. I called you twice."

"I got rid of my phone because Shizz kept calling and threatening me. What am I going to do about him?"

"Don't worry about him. We'll make a report with the district you live in and have them go after him."

We called the 18th District and had them send a couple officers out to the house, so we could report the Dodge Squad and their actions. It took a while for them to show up, but the officers eventually came out to the house and took the report. We let them know that there had been possible gang members in Dodge vehicles following us around, but honestly they didn't seem to care. They looked at us with uninterested expressions and gave the typical answer I knew they would.

"If you aren't able to truly identify the guys you think are following you, then there is nothing we can do," one of the officers said.

I was pissed off. This is exactly why I took matters into my own hands the first time. I told the officers to just document the incident and keep an eye out for the crew members.

The officers left and I stayed at the home to be with Tiffany and my Aunt Kim. A few hours passed and I ended up nodding off on the living room couch. It was a little after noon and I heard a loud knock at the front door. I was still half sleep, so it took me a little while to get fully focused enough to answer the door.

I stood up and began walking towards the front door, when suddenly I heard several gunshots going off. At the same time I heard the shots, I heard the sound of window glass breaking and screams. I dropped down to avoid being hit and yelled, "Get down" to Aunt Kim and Tiffany. The shots lasted approximately thirty seconds to a minute. When the gunfire stopped, I ran outside with my firearm to locate the shooters. When I got onto the front porch, I saw two black Chargers turning off the block. I ran back inside the house to check on my Aunt Kim and Tiffany. They were both upstairs and were not injured. They were hysterical at the time and I knew they were scared. I was completely frustrated and my heart felt like it was beating out my chest. It was difficult for me to catch my breath for a brief moment. I ran back outside and got into my car. I drove straight to Shizz Mack's home and kicked the door in again. I searched the entire home, but no one was there.

I remembered picking up Tiffany from a house at the corner of 67th Street and Greenway Avenue before. That house was like a little hang out spot for the crew and I knew he had to be there. While I was driving up 67th Street, I saw a bunch of Challengers and Chargers parked along the street. From a distance, I could see a group of people standing on the corner at the intersection. There had to be almost twenty people standing on the corner and some more sitting on the porch of the corner house. I drove right up to the corner, got out my vehicle and walked right up to Shizz

Mack, who was the only person I was focused on. I didn't say anything and punched him straight in the face. After I threw the first punch, his friends rushed me and we all began fighting. I was completely outnumbered and there wasn't much I could do. After I had been hit in the jaw by someone, I fell to the ground. Once I fell, they began kicking me.

I knew they wouldn't stop hitting me and I could barely defend myself. So out of desperation, I pulled my firearm from my waistband and began firing shots. The majority of the group started running, but a few of them got hit and fell to the ground. It just seemed like I blacked out with rage. I stood up and saw Shizz Mack on the ground. He was hit in the shoulder with one of the bullets. He was laying on his back and writhed in pain. He saw me walking towards him and he reached in his waistband for something. I pointed my firearm towards him and fired a shot. After that shot, I couldn't stop. The image of my abusive father popped up in my head and I continued pulling the trigger until my gun clicked empty. As his body lay lifeless on the ground, I could see the handle of a gun sticking out from his waistline. My adrenaline began wearing off and I felt the pain from the attack. I immediately got into the car and dialed 911 to report the shooting.

While in the car, the images of death and rage kept replaying over and over in my head. My father and Shizz were stuck in my head. The police and ambulance arrived on scene in minutes and swarmed the corner. They were picking up bodies, talking to witnesses and talking to me. Detectives arrived on scene and transported me down to police headquarters after the shooting, to be interviewed. When we got to headquarters, I sat in the interview room for about two hours before they came back in to speak with me. While I waited, I began to wonder about what just went down.

I knew I finally crossed the line and I was done. I planned to use my injuries as a defense to the shooting. Two detectives finally walked in the room and sat down. They looked at me and just didn't say anything for about five minutes.

"Can I tell you what happened?"

One of the detectives looked directly at me and replied, "You may want to get an attorney before you speak to us."

"I don't need an attorney. I want to tell you the truth. Those guys on the corner shot up my Aunt's house and I went up there to talk to them. When I got there, they attacked me and I fired my gun in self-defense. Some of them ran after the shots and one guy was on the ground and tried to pull a gun on me, so I shot him a few times."

"A few times? You shot the guy eight times. Did you know him?"

"Yes, I knew him. He used to date my cousin, but they recently broke up because he was abusing her."

"So basically this was a retaliation?" he said, as he tried to figure out my motive.

As soon as I was about to speak, Sergeant Domingo from Internal Affairs walked in. He stood in the corner of the room and didn't say a word. All he did the entire time was stare me down.

The investigating detective looked at me and asked, "So was the attack on your cousin reported?"

"No."

"Was the shooting at your aunt's house reported?"

"No."

"So let me get this straight. Two crimes allegedly occurred and you decided not to report either of them?"

"There wasn't time to report them. I had to handle them myself."

There was a brief pause in the room and both detectives looked at each other.

Sergeant Domingo stepped towards the table, looked right into my eyes and said, "I'm going to be very blunt with you, Mr. Townsend. We have more than ten eyewitnesses that say you came up and starting shooting into the crowd for no apparent reason. Most of them even knew about the incident you were involved in with your cousin, Tiffany. Not one person mentioned anything about you being assaulted at all."

"Well, obviously they're lying. You went and interviewed a bunch of gang members and their friends. Of course they're going to lie about what really happened and what's really going on. This is ridiculous."

Sergeant Domingo informed me that they had to place me under arrest and I snapped. I refused to place my hands behind my back because I didn't feel that I should be getting arrested. After hearing the commotion in the interview room, more detectives and officers ran in to assist in my arrest. Nothing could describe the anger I felt towards the entire department. I felt betrayed.

Officer Hoover Townsend was arrested and charged with the murder of Sean "Shizz Mack" Fordham, as well as three counts of attempted murder. He was terminated from the Philadelphia Police Department. The District Attorney offered him a plea deal for Manslaughter, in which he would only serve fifteen years. During the court proceedings, he refused to take the plea deal and decided to go to trial. He was subsequently found guilty of first-degree murder during a jury trial. Hoover

Townsend is currently serving the fifth year of his life sentence. He is currently in protective custody after several violent incidents he was involved in with King Cutta and other gang members inside the prison. Police investigated the shooting at Kimberly Townsend's home, but they were not able to link the shooting to Shizz Mack's crew.

CHAPTER THREE

Officer Dion Johnson was a three-year veteran of the Philadelphia Police Department. He was born and raised in North Philadelphia. In his teenage years, he attended Strawberry Mansion High School. After high school, Dion attended the Community College of Philadelphia, where he earned an Associate's Degree in Criminal Justice with a concentration in Corrections. Once he obtained his degree, Dion applied to become a Philadelphia Corrections Officer. He worked as a corrections officer for two years before applying to become a Philadelphia police officer. After completing the police academy in 2009, Dion served as a patrol officer in the Philadelphia's 12th District, which covers the Southwest section of Philadelphia. Shy and lonely by nature, Johnson found that putting on his uniform gave him a special appeal to some women—a heady new power that he assumed worked on all women... no matter what they said otherwise.

This is Officer Dion Johnson's story...

LUST

I spent two years in the Philadelphia prison system as a correctional officer. I was excited when I first started at the job because I now had a career and it was something new to me. I began my career in 2006 and left in 2008. During those two years, things got tough.

I worked at CFCF, which is the Curran-Fromhold Correctional Facility. Initially things were weird because I recognized dozens of inmates as people I went to school with, saw during social events and some of them were even former friends of mine. When I used to go to work at CFCF, it felt like I was an inmate too because we had no contact with the outside world during our shifts. We worked eight-hour shifts, but most days we were forced to stay and work mandatory sixteen-hour shifts. This schedule only left us with eight hours a day not in the facility and that was usually spent sleeping. The days off seemed to go fast and I truly believe I spent more time in the prison than I did at home.

Besides the hectic schedule, there were tons of scary moments in the jail as well. Several of my co-workers were seriously assaulted by inmates, which made me always keep my guard up. There wasn't much done to protect corrections officers and we had few ways to immediately defend ourselves from vicious attacks. All these factors helped lead to my decision to leave the prison system and join the police force. The police academy was smooth for me because I had already gone through similar training when I was in the corrections academy. Once I graduated, I was assigned to patrol the streets of Southwest Philly, which was a problem for other people but it didn't bother me. Certain districts were clean, up to date and pretty good work environments, but the 12th District was not one of them. We didn't even have parking lots for our personal or patrol vehicles. It was actually a disgrace when you think about it. Every asshole's favorite line was, "I pay your salary," like we worked in superb conditions. We were underpaid and we had to work out of buildings with deplorable structural conditions.

Southwest was a very busy and dangerous area of the city. I had a lot of fun working there because I basically got to do whatever I wanted. There were rumors going around that the 12th District was a "punishment district." People always said that all of the 12th District supervisors and most of the officers were always assigned there as a punishment, after they messed up or pissed off a high-ranking commander. This meant the supervisors didn't really care what we did. This was a gift and a curse. A gift because I didn't have that much freedom in a job before and now I did, but a curse because all that freedom gave me too much time on my hands. As most people know, when you have too much time on your hands, it usually leads to you getting in trouble. This was the case for me as well. I was a single man and my biggest weakness was a beautiful woman. I was locked down in an all-male prison for two years, so of course this was the case.

When I first began working, it was easy to see a gorgeous woman on a traffic stop or on a call and remain professional. That all began changing when women began flirting with me while I was working. I never had that type of attention before, so it felt great. I will never forget the first woman that caught my attention, because we dated for months after we met. Ashley Moore was her name and I met her in 2010. She was gorgeous and I actually met her at a traffic stop. I remember like it was yesterday. It was a typical morning during rush hour and she ran a red light. I wasn't really big on writing tickets, but I did stop cars to see if they would lead to something more. It was a normal stop at 52nd Street and Baltimore Avenue. She was driving a black Chevy Impala with dark tinted windows. I approached her car and literally stopped in my tracks when I saw how beautiful she was. I think she noticed this and giggled.

She looked me up and down and said, "Good morning, Mr. Officer."

"Good morning, ma'am, I'm stopping you because you just ran a red light. I'm going to need your license, insurance and registration card."

She handed me her information and I walked back to my patrol car to check it. It was crazy because she was even gorgeous in her license picture, which is rare since no one takes a good license picture. I checked out her information and it was all good.

I approached her car again and smiled. "Here's your information back. I'm just going to give you a warning for the red light and for your illegal window tint." We both laughed when I mentioned the tint, because she had to know that it was a clear violation.

"I bought the car like this."

"Yeah, I figured that. I would just make sure someone takes it off, because some cops will actually give you a ticket for it."

"Ok, thank you. I'll find someone to help get it taken care of."

"Ok, have a nice day" I said and began walking towards my patrol car. As I walked back to the car, I heard "Officer, wait." I went back to her car and asked, "Is everything ok?"

"Yes it is. I just wanted to give you my number because I think you're very attractive," she said boldly.

She handed me a sheet of paper with her phone number on it and drove off. At that moment, saying I was happy would have been a complete understatement. I was smiling from ear to ear and wanted to jump for joy. I couldn't believe a woman that gorgeous actually gave me her number. I put the number in my pocket and continued with my day. Throughout my shift, I wanted to call her but I was kind of reluctant. I never had someone give me their number while I was working before and I was not sure if it was acceptable or not. After my shift was done, I went home and relaxed. I began my night watching Sports Center on ESPN and scrolling through social media sites on my phone. I looked over at my work pants and remembered Ashley's number was still in there. I wanted to call her so bad, but for some reason I was nervous. I took the paper with her number on it, balled it up and threw it in the trash. I continued sitting there watching sports, but that got boring and I finally gave in. I took the number out the trash and texted her.

Me: *Hey Ashley, this is Dion the officer that you met earlier. Just wanted you to have my number.*

Ashley: *Ok. Mr. Officer, I got it ;)*

After sending the text, I only got the one response from Ashley. It was kind of disappointing, because I was expecting to have some sort of conversation with her. I just accepted the fact that she probably wasn't that interested and fell asleep watching television. The next day I headed to work and began my shift. I was patrolling in the area of 54th and Chester, when I heard someone constantly honking a car horn. I looked around to see what was going on and suddenly a car pulled up right next to me. It was Ashley.

"Hey, Mr. Officer."

"Hey what's going on? Let me find out you're out here stalking me," I said jokingly.

"Maybe I am. What are you going to do, arrest me?" She smirked.

"Maybe I will."

"Good, because I want you to," she said and winked at me.

That caught me totally off guard. "Where are you headed to?"

"I'm on my way to work."

"Well maybe I'll hear from you later."

"Or maybe I'll see you later."

After saying this, she drove off and I had to take a minute or two to register what she just said. I didn't know what to expect from her. She seemed to be interested in me, but I wasn't quite sure. All I know is that she was beautiful and I wanted to get to know her better. I continued working and around lunchtime, I received a text from Ashley.

Ashley: *Dinner tonight Mr. Officer?*

Me: *Sure, where at?*

Ashley: *You pick.*

Me: *Bahama Breeze. I'll pick you up around 8:30?*

Ashley: *Kk.*

Once again, I was smiling from ear to ear. This woman did something to me I couldn't explain. I got excited to see her, like I was a damn high school kid or something. My last true relationship was prior to beginning my corrections career and since then my only focus had been on work. I think it was the perfect time to try and focus on building a relationship with someone and I wanted that someone to be Ashley. My shift went by very slow, only because I now had plans. After work, I went home and relaxed before it was time to get ready. By the time 7:00 pm rolled around, I got dressed and stopped to get Ashley some flowers. I called to get her address and found out she lived in Sharon Hill, which is a suburban neighborhood right outside of Southwest Philly. I went to pick her up and she looked amazing. She was fly from head to toe and literally looked like a super model. The night was off to a good start.

The car ride to Bahama Breeze was very quiet. I was completely nervous and she was on her phone the entire ride. Once we got to the restaurant, we started warming up to each other. The night was amazing and I had a great time with Ashley. We got to know each other, had a lot of laughs and she seemed to be so perfect for me. The food was absolutely delicious and we both had a little buzz going from all the drinks we had. After the restaurant closed, we sat outside leaning on the car, laughing and joking some more. It began getting late and I decided to take Ashley back home. When we got to her house, I walked her to her front door and gave her a hug goodbye. I wanted to do a lot more, but I was being very respectful. It was hard because I was so comfortable with her and it felt great being around her. After hugging, I looked at her, smiled and began walking away. She immediately grabbed my arm, pulling me back towards her.

"I know you're not trying to leave without giving me a kiss."

I smiled and stated, "I wasn't sure I was allowed to."

She smirked and said, "You better stop playing it so safe, Mr. Officer. You have to take what you want."

She leaned up towards me and kissed me. Her lips were so juicy and whatever gloss she had on them tasted good. As we kissed, I felt her tongue slide slowly into my mouth and I couldn't resist but to grab her ass. She had on these tight pants that complimented her thick figure and I was eyeing her body up all night. We began making out in her doorway. It was getting hot and heavy. My hands continually squeezed both her ass cheeks and her arms were wrapped tightly around my neck. Finally we released our lip lock and she just looked at me. I could see the glare from the moon shimmering in her eyes and could smell the alcohol on her breath.

"You're lucky I have to work early in the morning."

I looked at her and smiled. I just had to pinch myself because I had to be dreaming. I could not figure out how such a gorgeous woman could be single. After

Ashley walked in her home, I left and just reminisced on the night. I could not get her off my mind.

Ashley and I went on several dates after the first and seemed to be growing closer. While we dated, I took my time with her and didn't rush anything. We made out a few times, but we didn't have sex until we were months into the relationship. I was working the evening shift and Ashley had gone to a happy hour event with some co-workers. She texted me around 11:00 pm.

Ashley: *What u doing?*

Me: *I'm working.*

Ashley: *Where u at?*

Me: *On 57th and Chester. Why, what's up?*

Ashley: *I wanna see u babe.*

Me: *When?*

Ashley: *NOW!*

Me: *Where?*

Ashley: *On Island Avenue near the airport.*

Me: *Ok. I'll be there in 10 minutes.*

I met up with Ashley in a business parking lot off Island Avenue. Her car was parked near a wooded area that was very secluded. There were no other vehicles or people in the area where she was parked.

I pulled up and asked her, "What the hell are you doing all the way back here in the dark?"

"I wanted some privacy. Can I get in the car with you Mr. Officer? Can I be your partner tonight?"

"Of course you can."

Ashley got out her car to come sit in mine. She was looking amazing once again. She was wearing this nice blazer that matched those tight shorts she had on and some heels. Her legs looked flawless and were just so thick. She got into the passenger seat of my patrol car and I couldn't help but to just stare at her.

"Hell, Officer Moore, you're looking mighty fine tonight."

She smiled and placed her hand on my right thigh. I watched as she looked around at all the things that were inside the patrol car.

"Show me how to turn on the lights."

I instructed her and she began playing with them, pretending she was really going to a police call. It was cute to me and honestly, I was just happy to be around her. She took off her blazer and revealed a very low cut shirt that showed off her perfect breasts.

"Damn."

She looked at me and then kissed me. As soon as our lips touched, I began getting erect. I immediately put my left hand on her breast and gently squeezed. As I did that, she firmly gripped my thigh. She was so aggressive. I then moved my hand down and began rubbing her smooth legs. My dick was literally pressing up against my uniform pants, ready to bust right through them. My mind wasn't on anything but Ashley at that moment. I tried to look around to make sure no one saw us, but I couldn't help but to stare at her body. It was as if my eyes were glued to it. Ashley continued rubbing my thigh and brushed across my hard dick.

She rubbed her hand across it and sexually said, "Wow, I'm impressed."

She unzipped my pants and pulled my hard dick out through the fly area. She rubbed it and asked, "Can I have it?"

"Of course you can."

She began taking her shorts off.

She had no panties on under the shorts, which turned me on. Once the shorts came off, I noticed that Ashley had a large tattoo of flowers that extended from her hip to her back. It was very sexy. Ashley sat back in the passenger seat and put her legs up. She began playing with herself while she looked at me.

"Do you want it?" she asked.

"Hell yeah."

She immediately climbed over the center console and got on top of me. I felt my dick slide right into her wet pussy. She moaned and I kissed her bottom lip to keep her quiet. She began riding me and I knew she felt how hard I was. She rode me very well, I was breathing heavily as she bounced up and down on my dick. Her creamy love juices were running down my dick, to my inner thigh. My eyes began rolling to the back of my head because the sensual feeling of being inside her was too good. The red and blue dome lights were still activated, which made the mood even better and hotter. The car was very cramped with equipment, so Ashley had her left leg straddled across the center console. I began to feel like she was in total control, so I placed my hands on her sides and squeezed her as I began to stroke back. I began stroking harder and rougher causing her head to hit the ceiling of the car every time I thrusted. She began moaning too loud so I had to place my hand over her mouth. I continued stroking her, removing my hand from her mouth and placing them both on her breasts. I pushed her upper body backwards over the steering wheel and I could see the top of her head almost touching the front windshield.

Ashley moaned and yelled, "Oh shit, you're about to make me cum!"

Hearing that made me more aggressive and I squeezed her breasts, pushing her harder against the steering wheel.

When I did this, the horn began honking and she screamed, "I'm cumming, I'm cumming!"

Thinking that the horn was going to draw attention to us, I attempted to look around but the windows were completely fogged up. I continued stroking as her pussy got wetter and wetter. I hadn't had sex in a while and I could feel my body preparing for an ejaculation. I continued stroking and suddenly I gasped loudly. I could feel the semen literally shooting out of my dick and into her pussy.

"Oh shit. That feels good." I continued ejaculating inside of her.

It felt like semen was continually coming out for about five minutes straight.

"That was so good," she whispered in my ear and gave me a tight hug, while my dick was still throbbing inside of her.

I didn't want to let her go, but I knew I had to get back to work. We sat there for about ten minutes holding each other. I continued to look around to make sure the coast was still clear and I cut the dome lights off. That had to be the best and most exciting sex I had in my life. I just happened to glance down at the clock and jumped up quickly. It was almost 12:15 am and my shift ended at midnight.

"Damn, I have to go baby. I was supposed to be off work fifteen minutes ago." I pushed her off me.

"Oh no, I'm so sorry. I didn't mean to hold you up." We both scurried around getting ourselves together and making sure she didn't leave anything behind. After she got dressed, Ashley gave me a sensual kiss and got into her car. I reached down to zip up my pants and they were soaked. There was a combination of both of our fluids all around the fly area and I had no way of cleaning it up. I drove back to the district and luckily no one noticed I wasn't back in time. I had to exit the car and cover my groin area with my uniform hat, so no one would see the front of my pants. I was able to drop off my patrol car and leave, without anyone questioning me. I made sure to leave the windows rolled down to air out the smell of sex that was left inside.

That night I got home, my mind was on Ashley and nothing else. I was falling for that woman and that little experience we just had was the icing on the cake. I wanted her and only her. I called her a couple times, but never got an answer. I ended up falling asleep and waking up to an offer to have breakfast, which I gladly accepted. I met Ashley at the Green Eggs Café in South Philadelphia that morning. We had breakfast and she told me how much she loved what we did the prior night. I had to express my concerns slightly because that was a big risk for me. If someone caught us doing that, I would be in a lot of trouble. Ashley seemed to understand and I was happy she did. What started out as breakfast, turned into us spending the entire day with each other. I loved every minute of being with Ashley, but there was one slight issue. Ashley's phone was ringing off the hook. It had to be ringing at least once every 10 minutes.

"What's going on? Why is your phone blowing up like that?"

"Nothing, just an ex that keeps calling me."

"Well answer the phone and let me talk to him."

"No, don't worry about it. You don't need to get involved. It's nothing major. I'll just turn my phone off," she insisted.

I didn't think much of the situation, and we continued with our day. We ended up going to the movies and stopping at some stores in Downtown Philly, so Ashley could do some shopping. While we were in Macy's, Ashley ran into two of her cousins.

"Hey Ash, I haven't seen you in forever," one of the cousins said.

"I know girl, it's been a while."

"What are you up to?"

"Nothing, just out spending the day with my friend," Ashley said, as she introduced me to her cousins.

That was a complete smack in the face to only be introduced as her friend. I didn't mention it at that moment because I didn't want to make a big deal of the situation in front of her cousins. About two hours passed and we were finally ready to go home.

As we walked back to our cars, I asked, "So I'm just you're friend?"

Ashley gave me a surprised look. "What do you mean?"

"You just introduced me as your friend to your cousins. I thought we were more than that by now."

"Come on, I know you're not going to get mad over a title. We have something special. We don't need a label to prove anything," she said and rolled her eyes.

That answer was not really what I expected. I planned on taking a step back from getting too attached to Ashley, because obviously we weren't on the same page. I was under the impression that we were building a relationship and apparently she only saw me as a friend. We both went home and I ended up signing up for an overtime shift at work. I figured if I stayed busy, I would keep my mind off Ashley. The shift I took was from 6:00 pm to 2:00 am. That shift was eventful; we were very busy so I didn't get the opportunity to call or text Ashley that entire night. That was exactly what I wanted. She didn't deserve my attention, if she was only just going to string me along. As I left work that night, I received a text from Ashley as soon as I got home.

Ashley: *Are you up babe?*

I didn't respond to the text initially, because I was still pissed about the situation. Instead I took a shower and tried to go to sleep. It was now about 3:30 am and I couldn't believe I was still awake. The first thing I did was grab my phone and texted Ashley back.

Me: *Yeah I'm up.*

Ashley: *Are you mad at me or something?*

Me: *No, why?*

Ashley: *Because I haven't heard from you all night.*

Me: *I wasn't sure if a "friend" was allowed to be texting you this late.*

Ashley: *Don't do that. I miss you.*

Me: *How much?*

Ashley: *Come here and find out how much.*

Me: *Ok.*

Ashley: *Can you please wear your uniform?*

Me: *Maybe.*

I was weak when it came to her. I got right up and started my way to Ashley's house. I got to her house around 4:30 am and all the lights were off. The door was already unlocked, so I went right in. I walked upstairs and saw her sleeping in the bed. I was somewhat confused because I thought she was going to be awake and waiting for me. I took off my clothes and got under the covers with her. Her skin was so warm and soft, which was perfect on this cold night. She was wearing nothing but a tank top and panties. I placed my left hand between her thighs and squeezed the warmth from them. Ashley flinched initially and looked back at me. I looked into her light brown eyes and she just smiled. I worked my cold hands up her warm body, causing goosebumps to form on her soft skin. I grazed my hand across her soft breasts, feeling the small bump of her hard nipple pressing through the tank top. She turned her head away from me and silently moaned.

My hands continued up, until they got to her neck. I squeezed gently and pulled her body closer to mine. She began moaning louder. I pulled down my underwear so she could feel the flesh from my fat dick pressed up against her ass. Once I did this, she began squirming and clinching her legs together. I reached into her panties and pressed my middle finger gently against her clitoris, causing her to flinch again and moan louder. I knew she couldn't handle it; she wanted me inside of her in the worst way. I wanted her too, but not just yet. As I massaged her clitoris with my finger, I began kissing the back of her neck and shoulders. Between the kisses, my wet tongue surprised her skin with sensual licks, causing the goosebumps to reappear on her body. I continued kissing and licking, working my way up to soft bites on her shoulder. As I did this, I could feel her soft lace panties getting moist. I pulled them to the side and continued massaging her now soaking wet clitoris. The moans continued and turned me on more and more. At this point, my hard dick was pressing her panties directly into the crack of her ass. She moved occasionally, repositioning her ass to ensure my dick was still in the desired location. I held back the urge to thrust my hard dick in her wet pussy, because I was enjoying the moment. The decision was hers to make when she wanted it.

"You're so warm," I whispered in her left ear before nibbling on the lobe.

"You're getting me hot, baby," she said in a very sexual tone.

This caused me to wrap my strong arms around her and squeeze her tight, forcing my dick to press up against her asshole. She moaned so loud, I knew she could not resist it any longer. She reached backed and squeezed my hard dick. I was so horny I felt pre-cum dripping from the tip of my dick when she squeezed it.

While she was still squeezing, she took her thumb and circled the pre-cum around the tip of my dick. This felt amazing and I was ready to enter her. I slowly pulled down her lace panties, exposing her ass and pretty pussy. She turned her head back towards me and smiled. She squeezed the shaft of my dick causing more pre-cum to protrude from the tip of my dick. This time she guided my dick towards her ass. The pre-cum acted as a lubricant and allowed my dick to glide through her ass cheeks. When the tip of my dick reached her asshole, she winked at me. She reached back and placed her left hand on my hip, pulling me closer to her. This allowed the tip of my dick to gradually enter her asshole. It was so tight and felt so good. The look on her face was priceless. Her head flew back and she moaned "yes" very loudly. Ashley grabbed the shaft of my dick once more and squeezed firmly. I could feel the pre-cum going right into her ass. She felt it too as she moaned "oh my god." The pre-cum moistened her asshole and I began slowly inserting the rest of my dick.

"You like it?" I asked and initially got no response.

She was too busy moaning and that was exactly the answer I wanted.

Suddenly she yelled out, "Oh it's so big! Give it to me."

This gave me a great boost of confidence and I began stroking her. Each stroke caused her to moan louder and louder. I just knew her neighbors had to hear everything that was going on. The sex felt so good, her tight ass squeezed every inch of my dick as I thrusted her backside. We went from sexing while laying on her sides, to sitting up and I was soon hitting it doggy style. I used her breasts as support, holding on to them while I ensured every inch of my hard dick entered her. I worked my right hand down towards her pussy, which was literally dripping as she continued to cum. I placed my hand directly over her pussy and massaged it in a circular motion while I continued stroking her tight asshole. Her love juices were running through my fingers and dripping on the bed. I had a lot of built in anger in me about the whole "friend" situation and I was taking it out on her asshole. I was fucking her long and hard and she loved every minute of it.

"Oh Mr. Officer, I've been a bad girl. You need to lock me up." She looked back at me while I was stroking her.

I pushed her off my dick and walked towards my clothes, which were piled up near her closet.

"Oh baby, put it on. Put your uniform on," she demanded.

I put on my uniform but left the shirt unbuttoned, to expose my strong chest and chiseled abs. I pushed Ashley back towards the headboard and stood over her on the bed.

"This what you want?"

"Yes, Mr. Officer. I want it all."

"Well Ms. Moore, you have the right to take this dick." I handcuffed her to the headboard.

"Make them tighter, baby."

I made the handcuffs tighter and she gasped. I sat back and looked at her sexy ass, as she laid there as my little prisoner. I spread her legs back and shoved my dick right into her dripping pussy. There was nothing gentle about my approach. Ashley appeared to like pain, so she got it rough. I lifted her legs and pushed them up towards her hands as I stroked. She was going crazy off every stroke. I squeezed her ankles so the feeling of my strong grip matched the tightness of the cuffs around her wrists. The look on her face was priceless. Her mouth was open and her eyes rolled to the back of her head, as if she was possessed. I looked down at my soaked dick as it continued to make Ashley go crazy. I felt Ashley attempting to pull her body away from me, as if she could not handle anymore. I sat back and slowly removed my dick from her pussy. She looked down at me as I did so. As I exited her, I placed my thumb on her clitoris and flickered it in an upward motion.

Suddenly she began screaming and fluid began squirting out of her and onto the bed. Ashley was having an orgasm. Her body was shaking and she was attempting to free herself from the cuffs, but she couldn't. I stood up over her once again and began masturbating. She looked up at me as she bit her bottom lip as if to tell me she wanted to taste what I was ready to give her. It didn't take long before I felt the pressure for an explosive ejaculation building up in my dick. I felt it on its way and I pointed my dick towards her pretty face. She immediately tried to reposition herself in preparation for what was coming. She opened her mouth and created a target for me to aim at. "Oh shit," I moaned as cum shot from the tip of my dick and onto her face and neck. It felt like my soul was being taken from my body, as I fell lifelessly onto the bed next to Ashley. She laid there for a while and closed her eyes, as my fluids dripped from her chin and onto her breasts. I was only able to gather up enough energy to release her hands from the cuffs, as they fell to her side and she prepared to go to sleep. My eyes became heavier as the seconds passed and the next thing I knew, I was sound asleep.

I woke up, only to feel my arm resting in a wet spot on the bed, serving as a reminder of last night's activity. I opened my eyes to see Ashley's beautiful face, which still had the remnants of my semen on it. She was still knocked out and completely naked. This is definitely one of those moments in time I wished I could just capture forever. I didn't want this moment to end, so I just pulled my body close to hers and held on tightly as she slept away. It was now around 10:00 am and Ashley was still sleeping. I ordered breakfast and had it delivered, so it would be there when she got up. I left when the food arrived, because I had errands to run. While I was out, I received a text from Ashley around noon.

Ashley: *Thank you baby. You're so sweet.*

Me: *No problem. You looked so peaceful this morning, so I didn't want to wake you.*

Ashley: *Why didn't you stay?*

Me: *I have a few things to do today.*

Ashley: *Ok. Well maybe I can see you later, if you're not busy.*

Me: *Sounds good to me.*

I continued running my errands and ended up meeting up with Ashley later that night. We went to dinner and hung out at her place for a while. Our relationship continued and things were going really well between us two. The only issue I had was the feeling that I was getting more attached to Ashley than she was to me. She never talked about making our relationship official and I never brought it up after the whole "friend" incident. In the winter of 2010, things changed between us.

There were several drug related shootings going on almost every other night in Southwest Philly. Our district received information that some gang members were plotting to take out a rival drug lord, named "Bizzy." Bizzy planned to have a big birthday bash at the Millcreek Tavern in West Philly on a Saturday night. Several officers, including myself, were assigned to assist 18th District officers with patrolling the area around the party. I could care less if a drug lord got shot, but the supervisors didn't want the hassle of dealing with a gang-related shooting or homicide. The party went on as expected and we ensured that everyone went home safe. We were all standing around outside the tavern waiting for the crowd to clear out at 2:00 am and a white Bentley coupe pulled up to the front of the bar. A guy got out of the Bentley and walked inside the tavern. I was speaking to one of the 18th District officers and he told me the Bentley belonged to Bizzy.

"Look, there he is now, coming out with all that jewelry on. He's so flashy," the officer said.

I looked up and saw a guy wearing what appeared to be some expensive clothes and a bunch of gold chains around his neck. He was walking with a beautiful woman towards the Bentley.

"I guess that's the girl of the night," the officer said, as he laughed. "Every time I see him, he has a new one by his side. Well, at least she's smoking hot."

I looked closer as the tall, thick woman walked up towards the car. Her body was very nice in a sleek red dress. She brushed her long hair away from her beautiful face and to my surprise, IT WAS ASHLEY. My heart shattered to pieces in my chest and I felt so betrayed. She was all over that guy and I couldn't believe it.

"Ashley!" I yelled out.

She looked up with a surprised expression on her face. Once she noticed it was me that yelled out her name, she hurried up into the passenger seat of the Bentley. The guy Bizzy stared me down as he got into his car and drove off.

"You know that girl?" the officer asked.

"Yeah, she's – umm – a friend of mine."

"Well, she didn't look like much of a friend of yours when she jumped in that Bentley." He laughed and walked away.

I started calling Ashley's phone, but of course she didn't answer. After about five attempts, it seemed she had turned her phone off. It immediately reminded me of the time we went out and someone kept calling her. She was playing me this whole time and I never saw it coming. I didn't hear from Ashley until she texted me two days later.

Ashley: *We need to talk.*

Me: *Nope. We have nothing to talk about. So that's why you never wanted to be with me. You had a man already.*

Ashley: *It's not like that.*

Me: *What is it like then?*

Ashley: *Me and you had a lot of fun together, Mr. Officer. That's all it was. We were never going to get serious.*

Me: *I see that now. Wish you would have told me that before now.*

Ashley: *Well now you know. We can still hang out sometime if you want.*

I never responded to her last text and really didn't hear from her much after that. I changed a lot after things ended with Ashley. I became somewhat cold hearted and bitter. I was once a man who believed in love, but that heartbreak made me only desire lust. I began dating several woman, but never got serious with anyone. I realized that Ashley didn't really like me; she liked the uniform. She wanted to fulfill a fantasy of being with a cop, as did most woman that flirted with me at work. Therefore, I decided I would take advantage of the uniform and I gave women exactly what they wanted. I would meet women while I was working and ask them out. I would occasionally have sexual relations in my patrol car, just for the thrill of it. This was exciting to me and made sex much more enjoyable.

I will never forget the night I met Tracy. I was working an overnight overtime detail and stopped in at the Wawa on Bartram Avenue, for a routine store check. It was around 2:30 am and suddenly I saw two beautiful women walk into the Wawa. They both caught my attention, but I played it cool and continued talking to the cashier.

"Well hello, handsome," a soft voice said behind me.

I turned around and saw a thick, Nubian queen standing in front of me in a tight black dress.

"Well hello, sexy. Coming from a night of partying?" My eyes focused on her cleavage, which was looking nice in that dress.

"Yup. It was my friend Shana's birthday and we went out to celebrate." She pointed to her friend who was walking up towards us.

I looked at the friend and asked, "Did you enjoy your birthday beautiful?"

She blushed and nodded her head yes. She was really cute too and had a shy personality, which drew me to her. I felt a gentle touch on my shoulder.

"Well I'm Tracy, what's your name?"

"I'm Dion."

"What's your number, Dion?"

"Wow, you play no games huh?"

"Not when I see something I want and you're definitely something I want."

I gave her my number and she actually called me immediately to verify that it was the right number. As they were leaving, I couldn't help but watch them walk out the store. They were both sexy and I definitely enjoyed the view.

"Damn, you're one lucky dude," the cashier told me, as he envied the attention the women showed me. I laughed and left the store. I began patrolling the neighborhoods again. As I began patrolling, I received a text from Tracy.

Tracy: *Are you busy?*

Me: *Not at the moment.*

Tracy: *Come see me.*

Me: *Where are you at?*

Tracy: *I live on Buist, right off 74th*

Me: *OK*

Tracy lived right near the Wawa. She gave me her address and I went right over there to see what she wanted. As soon as I began walking up the steps, the door opened. I walked into the house and Tracy was still in that tight sexy dress. Music was coming from a backroom and she walked towards the living room area. I sat down on the couch in the living room and made myself comfortable. I could hear a shower running and then suddenly stop.

Tracy began dancing in a very sexy manner in front of me. I watched intensely and enjoyed the show. I watched her curvy body fill that tight black dress. She began lifting the dress up which revealed her smooth chocolate thighs. She looked at me intensely as if I were a piece of meat. She turned around and began twerking to the music. Suddenly I saw Shana come from the backroom. She was only wearing a towel and was looking so beautiful. Her beautiful caramel complexion shimmered in the dim lights and her long, wavy hair dripped from just being washed. I never realized how gorgeous she was until now.

"Hey officer," she whispered in a very sexy voice.

She sat down on a chair across from me and just stared. It was something about her that turned me on. I could feel my penis began to rise and I had to continually adjust myself so it wouldn't show. Tracy could tell all my attention was on Shana, so she stood in between both of us and began undressing. She slowly took off that tight dress, which exposed her naked body. Her breasts were prefect and her dark nipples appeared to be pointing directly at me. Her pussy was completely shaved and appeared to be very moist. She kept her heels on and walked over towards me. In the background, I could see Shana still staring at me. It was hard to keep my attention on both of them, so at that particular moment I focused on Tracy. She stood me up and groped the front of my pants. Her hand rubbed across the hard imprint of my dick. In the background, I could hear the sound of radio calls being dispatched, but I ignored them.

Tracy unzipped my pants and dropped to her knees. By this time, I was fully erect and she could tell. She reached into my pants and pulled out my long, hard, fat dick. I glanced over at Shana, who was staring at my dick and biting her lip. I was so turned on from what was going on, I could feel my dick throbbing every five seconds. While I was looking at Shana, I could feel Tracy's soft lips kissing the shaft of my dick. She had my attention again. She looked up at me, opened her mouth wide and slowly slipped my dick inside. I could feel her moist tongue parading on my tip and it felt amazing. Her head thrusted back and forth, forcing my dick deeper down her throat. The only thing I could say was "damn," as I looked down at Tracy while she sucked me good. I grabbed the back of her head with my right hand and began stroking her mouth. She began moaning as I filled her mouth and she began squeezing my balls. I glanced over to make sure Shana was still watching and she was.

It appeared my actions were impressive to her because I could see her touching herself under the towel. She looked at me and smiled. I gave her a head nod, showing her I was interested in what she was doing and she acknowledged it. She slowly took off her towel and displayed her perfect body. Her slim figure was perfectly proportioned and was a beautiful sight. Both of her breasts were perky and her light brown nipples were pierced. My eyes slowly worked their way down to her tight abs and a thin strip of pubic hair, which led to her pretty pussy. She was working two of her fingers in and out her pussy as she watched Tracy suck my dick. I wanted them both and I knew I could have them. I signaled for Shana to come over to us. She walked over slowly and once she got near, I grabbed her waist and pulled her close to me. We began kissing, while Tracy continued sucking on me. This experience was entirely new to me. I never had a threesome before, let alone with two beautiful women. Shana went from kissing me, to kissing my chest, to kissing my abs and down straight to my dick. I looked down and both women were taking turns sucking my dick. I knew I couldn't keep this up for long because I would definitely cum before I actually got to fuck them.

I pushed them off and stated, "Hold on. It's not my birthday."

I smirked, lifted Shana up and threw her on the couch. I spread her legs and dove right in. I licked and kissed on her pussy lips, which made her quiver.

I pulled Tracy close and kissed her. "Doesn't she taste good?"

"Hmmm, let me see." Tracy joined me in pleasing Shana.

We both began eating Shana's pussy, at moments licking simultaneously and allowing our tongues to touch. We occasionally kissed while our lips were still making contact with Shana's pussy. Shana could not sit still. She would cum and I would lick it up and lick Tracy's lips. I worked my tongue up Shana's stomach and towards her pierced nipples. I sucked and squeezed them both while Tracy continued eating her out. I figured Tracy had enough of all my attention being on Shana, so she got up and handed me a condom.

She bent over and grabbed her ankles. "Now it's my birthday."

I grinned and gave her what she wanted. I slid my dick right in Tracy's pussy and she moaned so loud. I started off stroking her slow because my eyes were still on Shana. I smacked Tracy's plump ass and continued stroking, as she went back to eating Shana out.

"I can feel it in my stomach," Tracy yelled out, as I began pounding harder and harder.

It wasn't long now before Tracy yelled those magical words. "I'm about to cum all over your dick."

I could still hear the radio calls being dispatched from my portable radio, which was behind the couch. I was occasionally checking to make sure I wasn't getting any calls. I wasted no time once Tracy came. I put on a new condom and walked right over to Shana, who was still lying on the couch with her legs spread. I laid on top of her and began kissing her neck. She moaned silently in my ear as my tongue caressed her collarbone. I rubbed the tip of my dick against her pussy, teasing her while I nibbled on her nipple rings.

"Tell me you want it."

She looked right into my eyes and whispered, "I want it."

I squeezed my dick into her tight pussy and I could tell she wasn't expecting the size. I could feel my dick stretching out her pussy on every single stroke. Tracy came over and sucked on Shana's nipples as I continued stretching that pussy out. I tried to stay focused, but it was such a turn on watching the girl-on-girl action. Shana and I maintained eye contact, as if Tracy wasn't even in the room. I was giving it to her good and she was moaning louder than ever. I turned her around and began hitting it from the back. Her ass cheeks clapped against my hips on every stroke. I was pulling her hair and smacking her ass until it turned red. I felt her cum drip down my balls and I could feel her body going limp. I wasn't done with her yet, so I sat her up and made her get on top of me. When she began riding me, I laid back and watched her do her thing. She could barely sit on my entire dick because it was so big. I reached over and grabbed Tracy's ass. "Come sit on my face," I told Tracy. She gladly got up and put her moist pussy in my face. As I was eating her pussy and I stuck my tongue right up so she'd feel it enter her. All I heard was "fuck" repeatedly, as Tracy bounced up and down on my tongue, almost simultaneously with Shana who was still riding my dick. Tracy didn't last long before her body jerked and she jumped off my face.

"Damn, you really know how to eat this pussy, Mr. Officer."

Tracy was done and for a moment, it was just me and Shana alone. It was something bout Shana that made me want her. I pulled her close to my body as she continued riding. I began stroking back so she could feel the entire length of my dick, which made her go crazy. I knew at that moment I could have my way with her.

"Tell me you love me," I whispered in her ear, before sticking my tongue in it.

She ignored my request and moaned. I began thrusting harder and her moans became louder.

"Tell me you love me."

I thrusted my hips up and held my position, causing her to feel my dick filling her pussy.

"Oh shit. I love you."

I sneered because that turned me on. I resumed stroking her pussy, forcing her to repeat herself louder and louder. Although it meant nothing, Shana telling me she loved me made me hornier. I felt myself about to cum, so I stood up and put my dick in Shana's face. She pulled the condom off and began sucking my dick again. She looked at me as she continued sucking me and I ejaculated right in her mouth. Even after I was finished, she continued sucking me. Shana swallowed every drop of my cum and I fell back on the couch. That moment was absolutely amazing. Shana sat next to me on the couch and was all smiles. Tracy was sitting on the loveseat and was smiling too. I got up and put my uniform back on because I had to get back on the streets. As I walked out, I gave Shana my number so we could stay in contact.

After that night, I stayed in touch with Shana and Tracy. Shana and I hooked several times, but I wasn't too interested in hooking up with Tracy unless they were going to be together. Meeting women became a common occurrence when I went to work. I was focused on my work often, but I was addicted to the thrill and fun of having sexual relations while I was on duty. In the back of my mind, I knew my new mentality was the result of Ashley breaking my heart but I continued in my inappropriate activities. That all ended in the fall of 2011. I was working the 4:00 pm to midnight shift, it was a normal shift and not too busy. I was patrolling when around 11:30 pm, I saw a woman walking on 52nd Street towards Baltimore Avenue. My goal was to flirt with her a little and see what would come of it. I pulled up next to her and started a conversation.

"Where are you walking to, pretty lady?"

"I'm headed out of town for the weekend. I'm just trying to get down to the bus depot."

"What bus do you need to catch?"

"I just need to get to the 30th Street Bus Depot. You know down there where the Amtrak train is? I'm catching one of those buses that pick people up outside. I'm going to New York"

"Well, get in."

She didn't hesitate getting into the passenger seat of my patrol car and I began driving down towards 30th Street.

"So what do I owe you for this ride?"

"You don't owe me anything, but I'll take your phone number if that's ok."

"So once you get my number, what's going to happen?"

"We're going to get to know each other and maybe other things will happen."

"Well, how about we skip the number part and get right to the other things."

"That sounds like a great idea."

She reached over and unzipped my pants. I continued driving and she started giving me head. As I drove, her head bobbled up and down. The head she was giving me was sloppy and good. She deep throated me and her tongue flickered on the tip of my dick. She knew exactly what to do with it. I pulled up to the 30th Street Bus Terminal and she continued sucking me. No one was around at that time, so I wasn't too concerned with anyone seeing us. She was jerking my dick and sucking the tip at the same time. I came so hard and I ejaculated right in her mouth. She continued sucking me after I came, until I couldn't handle it anymore. She wiped her mouth with her shirt and sat back.

"So what do I get for that?"

I gave her an obnoxious look and asked, "Get for what?"

"What do I get for sucking your dick?" she asked again with an attitude.

"You can get my number, that's about it."

"I don't want that. You're going to have to pay up."

"I'm not paying you anything, so you need to get out."

"You're going to regret this," she said, as she got out and slammed the car door.

I drove back to the district to end my shift, when I heard a radio call come out for a Supervisor. The dispatcher came over and said, "Eighteen Command" (18th District Lieutenant), we are getting a call from Septa's Transit Police. They have a victim at the 30th Street Bus Terminal, claiming she was just sexually assaulted by a police officer."

I couldn't believe it. That chick lied and said I assaulted her. There was nothing I could do at that time, so I hurried back to the district and left work. I got home and began panicking. I received several phones calls from the district between 1:30 am to 4:00 am, but I refused to answer. I knew there was nothing I could say or do to get me out this situation. I got a pen and pad and wrote out the truth of exactly what happened with that woman, because I knew I probably wouldn't have a chance to explain myself later. At 08:00 am, I heard a loud knock at the door. When I opened the door, I was greeted by two detectives who informed me they were from the Special Victims Unit. I handed one of the Detectives the statement I had and placed my hands behind my back.

Officer Dion Johnson was arrested and charged with rape and related charges. He was terminated from the Philadelphia Police Department. After his arrest became public, other victims stepped forward to report similar incidents regarding having sexual relations with Johnson while he was on duty. During a jury trial, he was acquitted from the rape charges but was found guilty of Official

Oppression and Sexual Assault. He was sentenced to four years in prison. Johnson has several pending criminal cases against him and will not likely be released from prison if he is found guilty. He is currently serving his prison sentence at the Curran-Fromhold Correctional Facility, where he was formerly employed.

CHAPTER FOUR

Sergeant Jose Ortiz was a twelve-year veteran of the Philadelphia Police Department. He grew up in Brooklyn, NY and later moved to the North Philadelphia area of the city. Jose has been married for ten years and has two children. From afar, Jose was a great provider and fantastic cop, but when his stellar rise through the ranks landed him a coveted detective position, the cracks in his marriage erupted into an earthquake. With the hectic detective schedule, constant overtime and extreme stress, he and his wife kept growing apart. All the marriage counseling and pledges to fight for their relationship couldn't undo the worst damage when Jose was finally promoted to sergeant and became married to his job. While Jose took to drinking heavily during his rare free time to cope, his wife found comfort in other ways. When Jose found out his frantic reaction cost him not just his family, but the career he sacrificed everything for.

This is Sergeant Jose Ortiz's story...

UNHAPPY WIFE, UNHAPPY LIFE

I was a very ambitious young man. I grew up in a poor neighborhood and my family barely made ends meet. After the 9/11 attacks in America, I felt the need to do more for my family and myself. I thought about joining the military, but the opportunity to get into law enforcement arose first. When I joined the police force, my life changed drastically. I was determined to work hard because I was proud to have a career. I got married two years into my service and became a detective during my fifth year. When I first graduated the academy, everything was perfect. In my opinion, my wife Jennifer, was very caring and supportive. I would come home from a long day of work and tell her all about my day and our communication was very good. We lived a nice and stable life. She was a medical assistant at the time, but she always wanted to become a registered nurse. Her goal was to go to school part time and work towards becoming a RN. My goal was to move up through the ranks and have a successful career. We both were working hard towards our goals, but that all changed when Jennifer got pregnant in 2003.

While Jennifer was pregnant with our first child, things were great. We recently moved into a three-bedroom home in Northeast Philly and were excited to furnish the place. We had a lot of fun times decorating the baby's room and baby proofing the entire home. Around the time of the pregnancy, things were changing for me at work. I worked the overnight (12:00 am to 8:00 am) shift in the 26th District and was not home at night. I began getting several court appearances a month, which left me with very little time to spend with Jennifer and the baby during the day. I would literally work from 12:00 am to 8:00 am and have to be at court by 9:00 am. Court didn't end on most days until after 12:00 pm and by the time I got home, I had to try and get some sleep. My life was just work.

Jennifer was accepting of this in the beginning, because she had stopped working to spend time with the baby. I had to make money and doing overtime and showing up to court were the only two options I had. Once the baby came, I attempted to spend as much time at home as I could. Work began getting busier, which meant some nights we worked more than eight-hour shifts. The crime rate was rising and the work hours were getting longer. Jennifer understood that, but she was not too pleased about it. She would force me to call out of work, just to spend extra days at home with her and the baby. This was difficult because I was the only source of income and we were barely making ends meet. It was during this time I made the decision to take the test to become a detective. Jennifer supported this decision because we thought it would be a financial upgrade, which would help make up the difference of her lost income. We had no idea the workdays would be so strenuous.

By the time the baby turned one, Jennifer decided she wanted to go back to work to help with the finances. She applied for a medical assistant position at St. Christopher's Hospital and found a good day care for the baby. During Jennifer's first week of work, she began missing the baby too much and had a very hard time being away from the baby for eight hours a day. Jennifer and I talked about her being a stay-at-home mother and she ultimately decided that would be best. That decision was very hard on me because I was not in the financial position to comfortably provide for my family, on my own. After that decision, I worked twice as hard and began pulling extra overtime shifts. I was barely getting any sleep and was not spending enough time at home. Jennifer and I used to get into disputes because I needed help financially and she didn't want to go back to work. 2005 was a very rough year for me, when it came to my personal life. I was always stressed out and it was hard to communicate with Jennifer because we would just argue. I felt like being a good cop was making me a bad husband, because I was always at work. Things were very depressing for me until I received the news that I would be promoted to detective in 2006. Jennifer was ecstatic about the great news too. It rejuvenated our marriage and the thought of a slight pay raise was definitely what we needed.

In 2006, I began working as a Northwest Detective and it was very exciting. It was quite different from just patrolling the streets because I was more involved in the victims' lives during and after the investigations. I enjoyed what I did very much. The first year as a detective was easy. I didn't have a heavy workload because I was new, but I still worked the overnight shift. Things were great at home and I was able to make ends meet financially. Things between Jennifer and I were going really well, so well that she got pregnant again. We were excited to have another baby and we discussed the need for us to be supportive of each other. The remainder of 2008 was seemingly flawless. We didn't argue much and I was able to get adjusted to my new role at work. Although my role was good, the workload began increasing due to retirements, promotions, and transfers. It turned out that the detectives' schedule was a lot harder to deal with than the patrol schedule. I was not able to leave work while in the middle of investigations. That meant if I received an active job before 08:00 am, I was not getting off work on time. Unfortunately, this was the case during the majority of my shifts.

Each week I would work at least a twelve to eighteen hour shift, depending on the investigation I was working on. When I wasn't working on investigations, I was at court. I made a lot of money in overtime, but things became worse at home than they were before. Jennifer was more stressed out because she didn't have much support with the kids at home and never had any time to herself. We couldn't afford a nanny and the majority of our family still lived in New York. The only true support we had were her parents, but they worked fulltime. I would be angry because I was the one working all the time to maintain the roof over our head and it didn't seem good enough for Jennifer. I understood the fact that being a stay-at-home parent was a fulltime job in itself, but providing for the family was my number one concern.

When 2007 rolled around, we would literally argue everyday about the kids, the marriage, things breaking around the house and our future together. When I would come home, Jennifer wouldn't even ask how my day went or anything. I could not talk to her about certain jobs I was handling at work, because she was uninterested. Although I continued to do a good job at work, I was constantly stressed out. This led me to drinking alcohol almost every night. This was new to me because before I got married, I barely drank socially. Every time Jennifer and I argued, I would go in the basement and numb my pain with alcohol. I would pass out in the basement and not even sleep with Jennifer. Although this was temporary, it was my outlet and worked during that time. Our marriage was destroyed and I didn't know how to fix it. I remember on a spring day in 2007, Jennifer waking me up and yelling at me about drinking.

"You are a mess. Get it together, Jose," she yelled. I just laid there ignoring her. "I am not happy and things need to change.

"Things like what?"

"I think I'm ready to leave you."

I looked at the tears that were pouring from her eyes and it also brought me to tears. I didn't know how a love that was once so strong was now so broken.

"I love you Jenny, I just don't know how things got like this."

"You're never home with me and the kids, and when you are, you're down here drinking your face off."

"I have to work to keep the house and pay the bills. I thought you understood that. I have no support or help."

It was definitely hard talking to Jenny about the marriage, because we both weren't happy. We decided to schedule a marriage counseling session to help work on the marriage.

The counseling sessions were useless in my opinion. The counselor put all the blame on me and suggested I had an alcohol problem. Even when I tried to explain that our problems started before I began drinking, the psychiatrist didn't take that into consideration. He never once addressed the issues I was dealing with, which involved stress and financial issues. He only focused on what I was doing wrong and not on anything I was doing right. He painted a picture of me being an out of control alcoholic that wasn't doing enough to keep his wife happy. After three sessions, I decided not to attend any more and just worked on the marriage myself. Afterwards, things became calm in my household. They were not necessarily better, because Jennifer and I didn't speak often and really didn't sleep together. When I would be off from work and watching the kids, she would leave to go out with her girlfriends. When we were home together, I would rather be in the basement by myself and have a few drinks. Our marriage was not being repaired, but we weren't arguing anymore. Things were very manageable during 2007, but things definitely changed one night at work.

It was a summer night in 2008, and I was assigned a domestic violence case in which a woman discovered her boyfriend had cheated on her and they got into a fight. He punched her several times in the face and was arrested for aggravated assault. She was badly bruised. I initially spoke to the woman in the district lobby regarding the incident. She informed me that her boyfriend owned a barbershop/hair salon in the Germantown section of Philadelphia that was very successful. She mentioned to me that she had often suspected him of seeing other women, because she heard rumors about his behavior when she occasionally stopped in the barbershop. She would often catch him hugging up on women and being very flirty. She stated on the night of the incident, she went over to the barbershop after it was closed, because he never came home. His car was still parked outside the business when she arrived. She walked in the barbershop and observed her boyfriend having sex with a random woman on a couch in the waiting area of the building. She confronted the two of them, and she and the woman began fighting. During the altercation, her boyfriend choked and punched her several times, allowing the woman to run out of the barbershop half-dressed. That is when she called police to the scene. I told the victim I needed her to follow me to my desk to make a formal statement.

When we walked over to my desk, she stopped in her tracks and pointed towards my computer.

"Oh my fucking god, that's her. That's the woman that was in the barbershop with my boyfriend."

I looked over and noticed she was pointing to a picture of Jennifer I had next to the computer at my desk.

"What the hell is going on here? That's the woman that was fucking my man and you know her?"

"That's my wife, Jenny. Are you sure it was her?"

"I'm fucking positive. I fucked that bitch up. If that's your wife, call her right now so I can do it again."

I was in complete shock and it was as if I couldn't move. So many thoughts were running through my head and it all finally made sense. The reason we weren't arguing anymore, the reason we weren't having sex and all those nights she claimed she was going out with her girlfriends. It was all because she had some new love interest. I felt so stupid. I investigated crimes for a living and I couldn't even see the clues of what was going on in my own home.

The victim yelled, "I don't want this guy helping me. His wife is fucking my boyfriend, so I don't want him helping me."

My sergeant quickly ran over to see what the yelling was about. He spoke briefly with the victim and assigned the investigation to another detective, after she told him about Jennifer. Everyone in the room was staring at me and I was more embarrassed than I have ever been in my entire life. Just the sight of everyone's eyes glaring at me and people snickering made me sick to my stomach. I called Jennifer's phone more than ten times and she refused to answer.

"You need to go home and take care of this," my sergeant said.

I rushed home immediately with anger flowing through my veins.

I stormed into the house and observed Jennifer standing in the kitchen drinking a glass of wine.

"What the fuck is going on?"

She turned to me and said, "You know exactly what's going on and don't act like you didn't see it coming."

When she looked at me, I saw bruising and scratches on her face and neck. At that moment, I knew what the victim said had to be true.

"All you care about is work and not me. You don't tell me I'm beautiful, you don't do anything romantic for me and Brian does."

"Brian? Don't you mention his name in this house."

"Why not? Is it because I love him and not you?"

"You love him?"

"Yes and he loves me too. He told me that."

"Yeah, he's saying all these things while he has a damn girlfriend at home he is cheating on."

"He plans on leaving her, just like I plan on leaving you."

I was pissed off and hurt at the same time. She had no remorse for what she did and didn't care that I found out about it. I didn't know what to do, so I left. I went to a local bar to clear my head. As the shots of tequila kept coming, so did the tears from my heart. I looked around at different woman in the bar and felt like receiving comfort from them, but I couldn't. Even though my wife was not loyal to me, I could not seek revenge in that way. I continued drinking and the rest of the night was a blur to me. I woke up the next morning in the backseat of my car, which was still in the bar parking lot. I was hoping I just woke up from a bad nightmare and tried to erase the horrible memories from my brain, but quickly realized it was a reality. I didn't even return home that day. I went to a hotel and went straight to work from there. I could not bear to look Jennifer in the face, knowing she made the choice to hurt me the way she did. I decided the best thing to do would be to take some time apart to think about our future, if we even had one left. When I arrived to work that night, all eyes were on me. Nobody said a word to me about the situation with my wife and it was just an awkward feeling in the air. I sat at my desk and the only thing I could do was stare at Jennifer's picture.

While at work that night, the sergeant pulled me into the office to speak about the incident.

"Hey Jose, did you talk to your wife? Is it true?"

"Yes sir, unfortunately. She was sleeping with that guy and I had no idea it was happening."

"Are you going to be ok? I think you should take some time off to get your personal life back in order."

"But sir, work is all I have. I got nothing at home."

"Jose, you're a great worker, but you have to deal with the issues in your marriage. How can you come to work and help anyone, when you need help yourself?"

After hearing that, I took him up on his offer and took a week off work. During that week, my goal was to figure out what Jennifer and I were going to do. I went home to speak to Jennifer, but she was not there. I called her phone several times, but she didn't answer once again. I drove to Frankford where Jennifer's parents live, but she was not there either. The kids were at the house with her parents, but they wouldn't tell me where Jennifer was.

"Where the fuck is she at?"

"Jose calm down and tell me what's going on," said Jennifer's mother.

"You want to know what's going on? Your daughter is a fucking whore and got caught cheating on me. That is what's going on."

"Have you been drinking tonight, Jose?"

"So she came to you telling you I drink a lot, but failed to mention she was whoring around on me, huh?"

"You need to go, now. I'm not going to let you stand here and disrespect my daughter and your wife."

"Well, she disrespected herself by cheating on me and I am not leaving here without my kids" I replied.

She attempted to close the door on me, but I pushed it open. I ran in and grabbed the children. Jennifer's mother blocked my path to the door and began cursing at me. I pushed her out the way and ran to the car.

While driving home I suddenly saw the activation of red and blue police lights in my rear view mirror. I heard the loud roar of a police siren. I slowed down and moved over so the patrol car could pass, but it didn't and realized I was getting pulled over. I was stopped and two officers approached my car.

"How are you doing, sir. Do you have your license insurance and registration?" the officer asked.

"Yes I do. Can I ask why I'm being stopped please?"

"We received a call from your wife about you being involved in an incident with her mother. She is making claims that you assaulted her."

"This is unbelievable. I promise you the only thing I did was get my kids. I never touched that woman. There is a reason behind my wife's call. She just got caught cheating on me, so now she's mad. I'm a detective and you can call my sergeant and verify this information," I told him.

He told me to hold on and walked back to the patrol car with his partner. Waiting in the car was very hectic. I didn't know what was about to happen and could not believe Jennifer's mother would lie about what happened. While I waited, I received a phone call from my sergeant.

I answered the phone and said, "Hello sergeant, I got pulled over."

"I know. I just spoke to the officer's supervisor. You have some pretty serious allegations against you."

"What allegations? I went to my mother-in-law's house to get my kids. Nothing else happened sir. I'm telling you the truth."

"Well, your wife is claiming you went over there in a drunken rage, kicked the door in and assaulted her mother. She wants them to bring the kids back to her and she's threatening to press charges against you, if someone doesn't bring them back."

"Sarge, you know me. You know that isn't true. She is probably just trying to ruin me."

"Well she will succeed if you don't give her back the children."

As soon as I got off the phone with my sergeant, the patrol sergeant approached my vehicle and asked what my decision was going to be. I could not believe this was actually happening. My kids were crying in the back seat because they knew something was wrong. I told him they could take the kids back, although I knew I didn't commit a crime. They took the kids and allowed me to be on my way.

I could not bear to go home alone, to emptiness, so I went to the usual bar. Once I got to the bar, I began drinking my pain away because it was becoming very difficult to deal with everything that was going on. I didn't know what the solution would be, but somehow Jennifer became the problem. I spent the night drinking and eyeing up the crowd that was in the bar. I was approached by an attractive woman at the bar, who began conversing with me. I don't know if it was the alcohol in my system or the loneliness in my heart, but it felt so good having someone to talk to. This was a feeling I hadn't experienced in a long time. I briefly forgot about all the problems I was having and my only concern was getting to know her.

Her name was Rhonda. She was gorgeous, worked at a retail store and was out at the bar with some coworkers. Rhonda and I talked all night and she even introduced me to her coworkers, who seemed like very nice people. The attraction between Rhonda and I was so strong that I couldn't help but kiss her on the cheek at the bar. By the end of the night, I felt great and didn't want to leave. When the bar closed, I walked Rhonda to her car and she gave me a hug. The feeling of touching her was amazing, because I hadn't embraced a woman like that in almost a year. I kissed Rhonda on the cheek again and we gazed into each other's eyes. I could tell she was as attracted to me as I was to her. The alcohol gave me a little courage, so I leaned in and kissed Rhonda on the lips. She grabbed me and kissed me back. I was so turned on and I know she felt it.

She reached her hand down into my pants and grabbed my penis as we kissed. When she did that, I was totally caught off guard. I didn't expect that at all. I reached up her skirt and squeezed her firm butt cheeks, forcing her closer to me as we kissed. We got into the backseat of Rhonda's car and continued to make out. I laid on top of her and lifted up her shirt. I began kissing on her breasts and she began to moan. I gripped her breasts and the only thing I could look at was the wedding ring on my hand. I wanted Rhonda so bad, but I was still a married man. I put my left hand down and tried to ignore my ring. I began kissing Rhonda again to shift my focus. I got up and told her I had to leave. Rhonda had a look of shock on her face and I was confused as well. Although my wife made it clear she didn't want me anymore, I couldn't be with another woman while I was still a married man. I explained this to Rhonda and although she didn't agree with it, she had to accept it. Afterwards we both went our separate ways.

I drove home and felt like such a fool. I was still being loyal to a woman that didn't even care about me anymore. As I pulled up to the house, I observed my front door standing wide open. The first thought that went through my head was someone was trying to burglarize my house. Thinking it was a burglar in my home, I pulled out my gun and went inside carefully to look around. Nothing appeared to be stolen from the downstairs area, so I worked my way upstairs. I was not in my right mind and the room appeared to be spinning from the alcohol. I went into my bedroom and saw that all of the drawers were opened and clothes were on the bed. I noticed that all of Jennifer's clothes were missing and a note was on the pillow. The note read:

"Jose, I do not love you anymore. You do not know how to love me or the kids the way you should. You chose your career over your family and now you have to deal with that. I want to move on and find happiness and I think you should too. I have taken the kids and I plan on filing for divorce. Please make it easy for both of us. –Jenny."

I ran into the children's room and noticed all of their clothes were gone too. I was heartbroken once again. I dropped to my knees and began crying. I could not understand what I did wrong all of these years. The tears poured from my eyes like water from a faucet. At that moment, I lost everything and I didn't know how to deal with it. I raised my gun and put it up to my head. I wanted to end the pain at that moment and made the decision I was going to end it all. The room was still spinning and I quickly pulled the trigger. The loud bang rang in my ears and I fell to the floor. The gun fell from my hand and my head slammed on the floor. I began losing consciousness and for the first time in years, I felt at peace. To me, death was going to solve all of my problems. The feeling of a warm fluid running down, my head put me at ease and my eyes began closing.

I regained consciousness after about twenty minutes, to the sound of people talking in my home. I didn't know what was going on, I just saw several police officers walking around me. Some were jotting down notes and others appeared to be collecting evidence. I tried to get up but I realized I was strapped down to a stretcher.

The paramedics began taking me outside to the ambulance. My head was still spinning and I was so disoriented. I saw my sergeant in the home amongst the officers. He walked up to the ambulance before they took me to Jeanes Hospital.

"Jose, everything is going to be ok. You're going to get the help you need," my sergeant said.

I tried to sit up, but I was strapped down tight. The paramedics loaded me into the ambulance and didn't say a word the entire ride to the hospital. Once I arrived to the hospital, the doctor informed me I suffered a mild concussion during my incident. I asked him if I shot myself and he said I didn't, but I did have a graze wound on the top of my head. I was a complete mess. I couldn't keep my wife happy and now I couldn't even take my own life. A detective came to the hospital and filled me in on the details of the incident. He told me that I was so drunk, when I pulled the trigger I missed and grazed my head. When I fell over, I hit my head and passed out.

"We received a call from someone who heard a gunshot. While we were checking the area, we saw that your front door was wide open. When we entered your home, we found you knocked out on the ground. You were bleeding and a gun was right next to you. We could not tell what happened. Did you try to kill yourself?"

I knew if I admitted I tried to commit suicide, I would lose my job and would more than likely be committed to a mental institution.

"No, I didn't try to kill myself. I found my door open and when I was checking the house, I tripped and the gun must have went off."

He looked at me in disbelief and asked, "Are you sure? Because we found the note from your wife in your room."

"What note? I never made it to the bedroom."

He went into a bag and handed me the note. I read it and pretended to be shocked. He received a phone call from someone and informed he was leaving to allow me to rest.

I stayed in the hospital the entire night and was released the next morning. Although I could tell the officer didn't believe my story, he didn't push the issue. The next morning, I attempted to call Jennifer, but she never returned any of my phone calls. I ended up catching a taxi home from the hospital and my sergeant stopped by to check on me.

"What is going on with you, Jose?"

"Nothing sir, just going through a rough time right now. Jenny left me and took the kids."

"I understand. What she did to you was wrong, but at the end of the day, if you do not have it all together mentally it may be best for you to seek some professional help. I'd rather see you resign from the job than do something stupid like last night and end up getting fired."

"No sir, my career is all I have and I need it. I will work harder."

"It's not about how hard you work. It's more so about making sure we don't find you dead one day, which may have almost been the case last night."

Talking to my sergeant made me take into consideration everything I worked hard for. When he left, the brutal reality kicked in that I no longer had my wife or my kids. I began cleaning the home to keep myself occupied and I stumbled upon a fresh bottle of Cîroc Vodka in the kitchen. I shouldn't have been drinking, but I was depressed and I truly missed my kids. I poured myself a drink and went to lay down. I did a lot of thinking and decided I needed to focus on work right now and hope Jennifer would come back home one day. Throughout the next couple of years, I was able to manage work and be productive. I even passed the promotional exam to become a sergeant, which I was promoted to in 2012.

Once I was promoted, I was assigned to the 39th District. Although things seemed good at work, they were still a mess in my personal life. I was drinking more than ever, but I hid it well. I occasionally talked to Rhonda on and off, but the last time we spoke she told me she started dating someone. In November of 2012, I received divorce paperwork from Jennifer. I spent years trying to become a better man and she still wanted out. It was very hard to deal with. This forced me to resort back to my prior drinking habits. That night I went to a bar to have a drink, hoping it would calm me down. I drank a lot of alcohol that night and as I looked around the bar, I saw couples having a good time together. I could not get my mind off Jennifer and the kids. All I wanted was the opportunity to explain that I was a new man and tell her the news about my promotion. I just wanted to have some sort of contact with Jennifer, because I hadn't spoken to her in a long time. I made the decision to go to her mother's house to see if she was over there. After leaving the bar, I began driving to Frankford. I stopped at a red light and began nodding off. I was awoken by loud, continuous knocks at my driver's window. When I looked up, I saw two officers standing outside my vehicle.

I was unsure what happened because my head was pounding. I opened the car door and the officers began questioning me. I was unable to answer any questions due to my intoxicated state. The officers checked my pockets for identification and found my badge. After seeing my badge, the officers called their sergeant, who responded to the scene. When he arrived, he and the officers began speaking. I tried to focus on them but everything was spinning. After speaking with each other, they walked over to the car and asked me to step out. Once I did, I was placed under arrest. I could not believe what was going on. From what I remember, I repeatedly asked them why I was being arrested and they never answered me. They transported me to the police headquarters in downtown Philly and I knew exactly what was coming next. They tried to get me to complete the DUI investigation, but I refused to be cooperative. I could not believe I was actually arrested and I just felt my life was completely over now. None of the officers gave me an explanation, they just ignored me throughout the entire investigation. After refusing to cooperate, I was taken to the Internal Affairs building. I was placed in an interview room with nothing but a bottle of water, and was expected to sober up. While I waited in the room, a lieutenant in Internal Affairs walked in with a folder. He placed it on the table I was sitting at and opened it. Inside were photographs of my car and several other cars. It appeared that prior to the officers making contact with me at the light, I hit five parked cars. One of the cars had just parked and there were people still sitting inside when I struck the car. They are the ones that made the initial 911 call. There was no escaping this situation because my car was heavily damaged.

I looked at the lieutenant and stated, "I'm not saying anything unless I have a lawyer present."

He looked at me, smirked and said, "That's fine, because I don't plan on asking you anything. You're done."

He left the room briefly, returned with two detectives and a stack of papers. He placed the papers in front of me, and I observed it to be a Criminal Complaint, which charged me with Driving under the Influence, Recklessly Endangering another Person and other related crimes.

The lieutenant looked at me and stated, "Jose Ortiz, you are under arrest. You have the right to remain silent. Anything you say can and will be used against you in a court of law. You have the right to an attorney. If you cannot afford an attorney, one will be provided for you."

At that moment, my unhappy life was over.

Sergeant Jose Ortiz was arrested at that moment. He was charged and found guilty of DUI and related offenses. He was placed on probation, his license was suspended and he was ordered by the courts to enroll in a program that helps people deal with alcoholism. He was terminated from the Philadelphia Police Department. His divorce with Jennifer was finalized in 2013 and she retained full custody of their two children. Jose is currently trying to rebuild his relationship with his children. He has been sober for three years and counting.

CHAPTER FIVE

Officer Connor Mitchell was a six-month employee of the Philadelphia Police Department. He was born and raised in Philly, growing up in the Mayfair section of the city. Connor was born into a military family. His father and the majority of men in his family were Marines. Growing up, Connor always dreamed of joining them in the Service, but with his father so often deployed, Connor lacked the discipline he needed and sure didn't seem to be on the right track. By the time he was eighteen, Connor had been cited for several summary violations, from underage drinking to disorderly conduct by Philly Police. After high school, Connor managed to leave his troubled youth behind and enlisted. The Marine Corps gave Connor the discipline and structure he'd been missing, eventually molding him into a respectable young man. Connor continued this tradition of duty as a civilian by becoming a Philadelphia police officer. After completing the police academy in 2011, he served as a patrol officer in the Philadelphia's 35th District, which covers mostly the Olney and Logan sections of the city. Proving that no good deed goes unpunished, Connor's career nearly came to an end after only a few months when he exposed a corrupt, high-ranking supervisor and his cohorts of dirty cops.

This is Officer Connor Mitchell's story...

SNAKES IN THE GRASS

I had a rough career with the Philadelphia Police Department. I always felt like I was different from the other cops. To me, it seemed like most of them wanted to be cops since they were little kids. It was different for me because becoming a cop was the best opportunity life had to offer me, after the military. Although the majority of my family were military men, none of them were ever interested in law enforcement. I barely had passible grades in high school and I never went to college, so I didn't think I qualified to be an officer. I got lucky because at the time I applied, the requirement was only having a high school diploma and not college credits. I grew up in a low-income neighborhood, with just my father and he was away a lot with the military. When he was away, I would stay with my grandmother and she would take care of me. As a teenager, my friends and I always got harassed by cops. Every encounter I had with the police was negative and those encounters became more frequent.

I needed some type of discipline in my life, so my dad thought it would be best if I joined the Marines. Joining the Marines was honestly the best decision I made in my life. Initially it was a reality check for me because I was not used to authority, but I soon realized that I couldn't fight my way out of that situation. I was deployed overseas, where I lost many friends during the war. When I returned from deployment, I applied with a few friends to become a Pennsylvania State Trooper. During the hiring process with the Troopers, I didn't advance through the process because all of the nonsense I was involved with in my past and my lack of credentials. After being denied by the Troopers, I applied to the Philadelphia Police Department. After a thorough background check, I was grateful to hear I would be able to attend their police academy.

Starting the academy was smooth because I was used to the military discipline, but dealing with other police recruits was difficult for me. I often clashed with my classmates because I felt they were weak and didn't deserve their positions. I was in a class with men and women, who some have never been punched in the face before but they feel they could protect and serve in one of the most dangerous cities in the country. They were little snobs in my recruit class that had all these preconceived notions about the job, because they all had friends and family members that were cops. It was hard for me to get along with most of the recruits because I came from the streets and understood what really goes on in my city. Every time I heard some of my classmates discussing criminal procedures, they reminded me of the cops that used to harass me in my past. I just knew the same plague of stereotypical cops from the past were passing their bullshit down through generation after generation of new cops. After a very long eight-month academy, I was finally ready to hit the streets. We graduated in the summer of 2012.

I was assigned to the 35th District, which actually covered one of the neighborhoods I used to hang out in when I was younger. The department had all the rookies walk a foot beat when we first graduated the academy. The mission of the foot beats were to provide a constant police presence in the most dangerous areas of Philadelphia. They stuck me in the area of 5th Street and Tabor Road. During the first week of my beat, they partnered me up with Officer Angel Reyes. Reyes was from the BadLandz section of North Philly and spoke Spanish, which helped a lot. Reyes and I had a lot in common. We were both single, young, had no kids, had military experience and were the first people in our families to become cops. We ended up becoming close friends and I felt like he really had my back. During the first few months walking the beat, we would always see friends and other people we know who were very surprised to see that we had become cops. I personally lost tons of friends, once they found out I became a cop. I was so pissed that people could not look past the uniform and see that I was the same person they grew up with back in the day. As the months passed, I really didn't associate with anyone I once called a "friend." They all stopped calling and never wanted to hang out, so I did the same. Reyes related to this because he had many friends he grew up with join a popular Latino street gang in Philly and they all stopped associating with him completely, until they needed favors. We would both get occasional calls from other cops, in reference to people trying to get out of tickets or arrests by saying they knew us. This was one of the most annoying parts of the job.

I will never forget our first arrest. We were getting several complaints from residents in the neighborhood about a drug house in the area. The house was abandoned and local drug dealers used it as a hangout spot and a place to perform their transactions. Due to the drug house, neighbors were scared to let their children out of the house to play because they didn't want them exposed to all the criminal activity that was going on. Reyes and I went to some of the veteran cops and our sergeant to let them know what we wanted to do.

"Sarge, can we go in and raid the drug house on Wellens Street?"

"It's a waste of time; you are never going to catch anyone going in or out that house. They are going to see you before you see them."

"But Sarge, we aren't doing anything now except walking around. We want to get in some of the action and help out the neighborhood."

"Youngin', you have a lot to learn about this job. Be glad the only thing you're doing is walking around because you will have a career full of nonsense once you get off that beat."

I could not believe this, no one wanted to help us at all. We had to continue walking around the neighborhood and just watched as crime slowly took over. The residents that once asked us for help, saw us doing nothing about the crime and they didn't like it at all. Night after night we would hear calls for shootings and robberies being dispatched and we stood on street corners as patrol cars flew by us with their lights and sirens. All we wanted was to help out, but we could not do much on this foot beat.

"This is bullshit man, I can't believe I waited to get out the academy for this shit," Reyes said.

"I know right we aren't doing anything. I signed up to fight crime not to walk laps around the same neighborhood every day."

"Well let's hit the drug house."

"Naw man, you heard what the sergeant said. We aren't going to get anything if we hit it."

"Well if we aren't going to get anything, than let's hit it. There's nothing to lose."

He actually made a very valid point. I figured if the sergeant was right, then the house would be empty anyway. Therefore, we hit it.

It was around 7:30 pm in July of 2012, the night we decided to hit the house. We slowly crept up to the rear of the house from the alleyway. The windows were boarded up, so I couldn't tell if any lights were on. I put my ear to the rear door and heard music and voices coming from inside. Reyes and I didn't know what we were getting ourselves into, but the thrill of it all was unexplainable. I turned the knob on the rear door, which was unlocked. I slowly opened the door, to avoid anyone inside hearing it. I peeked in and observed the doorway to be empty and a dim light coming from the actual basement. Reyes and I walked inside the basement area and stopped in the doorway. We were standing in the doorway and I heard footsteps coming from upstairs. It sounded as if someone was just pacing back and forth. I also heard a male's voice coming from the basement room where the light was coming from.

"Yo. So what you doing this weekend? I want to see you. You're always bullshitting me when I come around," the voice said.

I looked at Reyes and said, "He's on the phone. Let's get him."

Reyes had an eager look on his face and gave me a head nod that showed he agreed with what I wanted to do. We ran in the room and announced "Police, don't move." As I looked at the male, I observed him sitting on the floor. He appeared to be packaging a white powdery substance, which was discovered to be cocaine. Once he saw us, he grabbed a crate and threw it in our direction. He tried to run upstairs, but Reyes grabbed the guy's shirt and they began wrestling on the step. The guy almost broke free, but we jumped on him and placed him in handcuffs. From upstairs, you could hear footsteps running around and the front door suddenly open. The suspects that were upstairs quickly ran from the home when they heard us. I told Reyes to stay with the person we arrested and I went upstairs to search the rest of the house. I drew my firearm and slowly crept up the steps. I was moving in a stealthy way to avoid being heard. Everything was dark, besides another dim light on upstairs. I checked the rest of the house and it was all clear. It was obvious that the house was frequently inhabited. There was a large amount of marijuana upstairs in the kitchen area and some cash. It was obvious whoever was up there wasn't able to gather all their products before running out.

The procedure for making an arrest while on the foot beat was to call for two patrol vehicle units, one to transport the prisoner back to the district and one to transport us. Reyes transmitted over the radio for two patrol cars to come to the scene. The first car pulled up and two veteran cops asked us what we had. We are beyond excited and told them exactly what we did and everything we found inside the drug house. They seemed to be helpful and offered to transport the prisoner back to the district for us. Our sergeant was off, so the normal patrol sergeant showed up and stated the crime scene had to be held, so that detectives could come out to photograph and collect all evidence. The sergeant ordered us to the hold the scene and we waited almost two hours for the detectives to come out. The detectives took a few hours processing the scene and offered us a ride back to the district, which we accepted. When we got back to the district it was now after 12:00 am, which meant the shifts had changed and different officers were now on duty. We asked the detectives how we should write up the initial report and they informed us all reports were already completed.

"That can't be, because we arrested the guy and we haven't written any report yet" I told the detective.

"That's weird. Officers Morton and Battles wrote up the report and processed the prisoner. It's their arrest."

I immediately got pissed off and couldn't believe we just did all of that hard work and those cops stole our arrest. Reyes went to the on duty sergeant and explained the situation.

The sergeant laughed and stated, "You should have never given them your prisoner. This type of stuff happens all the time to new guys. You rooks will learn not to trust cops." That night I went home, I couldn't believe what just happened. I didn't know who to go to about the situation or if anything could actually be done. How could they write an arrest report and they weren't even the officers that arrested the person? Isn't that illegal?

I couldn't even sleep once I got home. I stayed up all night and somehow alcohol became my companion that night, to take my mind off the events that took place at work. I called Reyes a few times but he didn't answer. I didn't have anyone to really talk to about the situation, so I had to talk to the bottle of Amsterdam Vodka I was drinking. So many thoughts ran through my head. Should I quit the force? Could I transfer to another district? Were all cops like this? Did their sergeant allow them to do this? I was determined to have this situation corrected one way or another.

The next evening I went to work and approached those officers in the locker room.

"What the fuck was that about. Why did ya'll steal our arrest?"

Officer Battles got in my face. "Rookie, you better get the fuck out my face before I break yours."

Other officers were in the locker room, but no one seemed interested in our little dispute.

"I want to know why ya'll stole our arrest last night."

After asking a second time Officer Battle threw a punch at me, that missed. I grabbed him and we began fighting. We were tussling, slamming into lockers and I was trying my hardest to knock his head off his shoulders. During the fight his partner, Officer Morton, also began punching me. I was fighting these two guys and no one jumped in to break it up or anything. I fell to the ground and they continued punching and kicking me. Their supervisor was Sergeant Wallace. He was a very strict guy and never spoke to any of the rookies. He acted as if we didn't exist when he would walk by us in the district.

Sergeant Wallace heard all the commotion, walked into the locker room and yelled, "What the hell is going on in here." Everything stopped when he walked in.

"The Rookie took a swing at me sir. He is out of control," Officer Battles said.

"He's lying," I yelled. "He swung at me first and then they jumped me."

Sergeant Wallace went around the locker room and began asking other officers who started the fight and they all indicated that I did. Of course, they would all blame the new guy instead of one of their own. I could not believe the betrayal that was going on right in front my face.

Sergeant Wallace ordered me upstairs to his office.

"Do you know what a probationary employee is young man?"

"Yes I do sir, it's what I am. An officer that graduates the academy is on probationary status for a year."

"Exactly it means you are an at-will employee that can be fired at will. You do not receive union representation for anything, so I suggest you get along with the veterans at the district because you are already starting your career off on the wrong foot."

"But sir, it wasn't my fault."

"I don't care what beef you have with Morton and Battles, but you need to let it go."

"Well as a supervisor, it would be nice if you were unbiased in this situation, instead of just taking your guys side."

He snapped on me. "WHAT. Who the hell do you think you're talking to like that. I will have you shipped to another district with just one phone call boy. You need to learn the rules of this job."

"I meant no disrespect, sir. I would just like a little support," I said in a shaky voice.

"Support? You had just better be glad I don't knock you out myself after what you just said. Now get the hell out of my sight."

After speaking with him, I got sent home for the day. I was still in disbelief about what took place. My only concern was getting revenge on those guys ASAP. I didn't know how or when, but I definitely wanted to get them back. Reyes called my phone a few times to check on me but I didn't answer. I didn't want to speak to anyone from that job. I spent my mandatory day off hitting the gym and running errands. I was so angry, I was prepared to fight the next day, but I knew that wouldn't sit right with Sergeant Wallace or any of the other supervisors at the district.

I went to work the next evening with a clear head. Reyes and I were assigned to our foot beat back on 5th Street. The night was fairly quiet up until 1:00 am. We responded to a fight at DejaVu bar which was located on the 5900 block of 5th Street. The paramedics were also dispatched, so I knew things were going to be bad. We ran up to the bar and I observed a large crowd gathering around a car in the parking lot. The car was a newer model silver Honda Accord. Initially I couldn't see what was going on because too many people were in my way, but they slowly began clearing a lane for me to approach. Suddenly, my eyes focused on a large amount of blood that was on the driver's door. The blood appeared to have a trail, which my eyes carefully followed. The trail led to an unconscious male that was lying beside the vehicle. I immediately ran over to him, when people began explaining what happened. People were screaming and yelling at us. It was complete chaos.

"They attacked him."

"He just got jumped."

“What took you guys so long to get here?”

“Where the hell is the ambulance?”

"Two guys jumped him and smashed his head on the window."

For some reason the last comment got my attention and my eyes began scanning the scene. There was shattered glass under the victim and it was clear it came from the driver side window of the Honda. The victim was breathing, but he was completely unresponsive. I notified the dispatcher to have the paramedics expedite their travel, to get this guy to the hospital soon. If we had a patrol car, we would have already scooped him up and drove him to the hospital ourselves. Reyes and other responding officers were trying to calm the crowd down and get some further information, while I stayed by the victim's side.

I looked up at a girl that was crying right over my shoulder and asked "where are the guys that did this?"

"They left after they attacked him."

"Who are they?"

"Just some guys that came into the bar. One of them was trying to hit on me, but I wasn't interested. He was being too persistent and that's when my friend Greg (pointing to the victim) intervened and told him to stop. Greg is a really good guy, he bartends here and doesn't mess with anybody. My name is Courtney and I always come visit him here. We're like best friends. He walked me to my car and they jumped him out of nowhere. I tried to help but they pushed me down to the ground," she said as she sobbed.

When she was talking, she showed me her right forearm, which was all scraped up, and bleeding.

“This is what happened when I fell to the ground.”

I realized why she was crying so hard, because she was probably the reason Greg got attacked.

"Where did they go?" I asked, so I could put their description out to other responding units.

"I don't know. They ran and got into a big white pickup truck and drove off" she replied. "Oh yea, one of the guys was saying he was a cop but I think he was lying because he didn't look like one. However, I heard him say something like that to another girl inside the bar. It was like he was using that as a pick up line or something.”

I really wanted to know what a cop "looks like" for her to think he wasn't one, but I just had to go off the information she gave me. The paramedics finally arrived on location and began treating Greg and Courtney for their injuries. I notified the dispatcher that we would need detectives to come to the scene and photograph the Honda, which turned out to be Courtney’s car.

Reyes ran over to me and said, “Yo, I got the tag and it comes back to a 2015 Ford truck, registered to Adam Nesmith and he lives on Torresdale Avenue.”

I immediately went over the radio to give the dispatcher a message.

“Thirty Five Foot beat Three to Dispatch.”

“Thirty Five Foot beat Three proceed.”

“Dispatch, the suspects left in a newer model white Ford F-150. It’s registered to a home on Torresdale Avenue, can you contact the district the residence is in and have them send some officers to the house?”

“Thirty Five Foot beat Three, ok. We will contact them now.”

Reyes and I remained on the scene for a while speaking to different witnesses and I received a phone call from a number that didn't look familiar. I answered the call and it was Sergeant Wallace. I had no idea why he was calling my phone, but the first thing I thought was he was probably going to send Morton and Battles to steal another one of our arrests.

"Hey rookie, did you guys clear from that job yet?"

"No sir, we're waiting for the Detectives to show up."

"They aren't coming out there."

"What do you mean they aren't coming out here," I asked. "We have an aggravated assault and tons of witnesses, why wouldn't they come out here?"

"Because it was just a fight between two dudes and one lost. Apparently the guy that's on scene with you was the aggressor."

That statement really confused me because he didn't even come to the scene, so how would he know anything about what occurred. He also thought the victim was still on scene, so where was he getting his information?

"Sir my victim was not the aggressor and he was taken over to Einstein Hospital because his whole head is busted open. I have an eye witness who can identify the suspects."

There was a very awkward silence and he finally said, "Listen the detectives aren't coming out there because you have nothing. I already spoke to the supervisor in the 8th District and the owner of that truck gave his side of the story. I'm sending some officers over to pick you two up; you're going to walk a beat at Broad Street and Olney Avenue for the remainder of the night."

He immediately hung up on me and I looked at Reyes with confusion all over my face. I didn't know what the hell was going on.

"What's wrong?" Reyes asked.

"Sergeant Wallace is sending us to Broad and Olney and he said the detectives aren't coming out."

"But why? What about the scene? Do the detectives know what we have out here?"

"No man, we're getting played by the sergeant. Something ain't right."

No sooner after I said that, a patrol car pulled up. I looked inside the car and it was Morton and Battles.

"Get the hell out of here," I said to them.

"Fuck you say to me rookie?" asked Morton as he hurried out his car and got in my face.

I looked around saw a ton of people still standing around from the bar and they were watching us. They began taking their phones out, once they saw how aggressive he was towards me.

"Go ahead you little bitch, what the fuck are you going to do. All eyes are on you right now so, make a move."

He looked around and realized I was telling the truth, so he backed down and got back in the patrol car. I became concerned when he began laughing in a very sinister way. He immediately got on his phone. I knew exactly who he was going to call and just a few minutes later that person pulled up.

"Get in the car, now!" Sergeant Wallace ordered.

Reyes and I got in the back of the patrol car and he drove us back to the district. The entire ride Sergeant Wallace's beady eyes were focused on me through his rear view mirror. I felt that he was attempting to bully me so I kept a stern glare on my face, while I focused my eyes directly on his. When we arrived to the district, there was a man standing inside the sergeant's office.

It was apparent he was waiting for us because his eyes were locked in our direction as we entered the office. We sat down as he stood next to Sergeant Wallace. He was wearing the department's dress uniform and his badge was decorated with several accommodation pins. He was sharp. His haircut was high and tight, face was properly groomed and he was wearing a pair of knee high leather boots that appeared to be spit shined.

"Hello gentleman. I am Captain Nesmith with the Highway Patrol Division."

As soon as he said that, I jumped up from my seat and looked for his uniform nametag, which confirmed his last name.

I looked directly at him and stated, "Adam Nesmith." I could see the expression on his face had changed and his should began to slouch.

"That is my son. He is a very good kid. He will be one of us soon; he graduates the police academy in a few months."

It now made sense and the pieces of the puzzle were being put together in my head. That explained why the detectives never showed up and why they wanted us away from the crime scene.

I became frustrated and stated, "Your son assaulted a man and woman tonight and put them both in the hospital. Your son is not a good kid; he's a suspect in an aggravated assault that occurred tonight."

"I don't think he is," Captain Nesmith said in an arrogant manner. "The sergeant here told me the detectives aren't working on any assault cases from tonight. All you have is a drunk bartender that tried to attack my son and fell after my son defended himself. It doesn't seem like a crime occurred here officer."

"That's a lie and you know it," I yelled. "There are plenty of witnesses and we talked to them all. Your son and his friend attacked the bartender for no reason."

He paced around the room a few times, while Reyes and I watched him closely. Reyes stayed quiet the entire time, as he felt the tension in the room.

"Who do you know?"

"What do you mean?"

"Who do you know? Do you have any family or friends in the department?"

"No, I don't know anyone."

He looked at Reyes and asked, "how about you, do you know anyone?"

Reyes shook his head no and Captain Nesmith smirked.

"Well I'm going to tell you this now before you two find out the hard way later in your careers. You will get nowhere in this department unless you know someone. No matter how hard you work, you will never get into a special unit or transfer to a district of your choice unless you know someone important. I am someone important. If you two make the right decision in the next minute or two, I will owe you a favor when the time comes and trust me you are going to need one."

"With all due respect Captain, I don't want any favors from you." He gave me the most evil look I ever received in my life.

"Ok you listen to me officer. I have the power to end your career before it gets started. Don't force me to do that. I'm being nice by giving you a chance to step away from this incident, but don't you dare try to force my hand," Captain Nesmith said in a very authoritative voice.

I knew at that moment my back was against the wall. I had two of my superiors in the room, ordering me to lie about someone being assaulted. I couldn't even believe this, it all seemed unreal. Staying in this room and looking at them was irritating me, so I got up and walked out.

I walked in the control center of the district and began writing the incident report. In Philly, we wrote the initial incident on a 75-48 form and submitted it in the control center to be entered and approved by the supervisor. As I was writing the report, Reyes walked in and put his hand on my shoulder.

"Just let it go. They're out to get us." Reyes said to me.

"I can't let this go. It ain't right and we would be just as bad as them if we give in. What if that was your brother or friend out there bleeding from the head? Would you feel the same way you do now?"

I looked over his shoulder and saw Sergeant Wallace and Captain Nesmith walking out of the building. They stared me down and I just scowled right back at them, making sure they saw the report in my hand. Reyes looked back at them and I could tell by his face that he was worried. He was just a young man that was concerned about keeping his job, so I wasn't too mad at him. I understood why he just wanted to give in, but I wasn't going to let that happen. I finished the report and submitted it.

Reyes and I began talking, when the corporal said, "Fellas, you just submitted a report that is already in the system."

I walked over to her and stated, "That's impossible. We just took the report and nobody else was out there with the victim."

"Hold on," she said and began typing away at the keyboard. She looked closely at the screen and told us "It looks like Officer Battles submitted the report and it was approved by Sergeant Wallace about an hour ago."

This could not be happening. It just went from a bad dream to a nightmare. I went to the Lieutenant's office to speak with him about this situation, but the door was locked and I didn't see him all night. I was stuck with no other options left. What was I to do? Whom could I trust? Who would listen a brand new rookie over a bunch of seasoned veterans and supervisors? There was literally nothing I could do. Our shift was ending and I had a plan. I was going to go over to Einstein Hospital and tell the victims everything that was going on, so maybe they could do something about it. Reyes and I went to the locker room to change and I told him about my plan.

"Let's go to the hospital."

"And do what?"

"We need to talk to the victims. We need to do our job."

"We aren't about to have any job to do. You heard what Captain Nesmith said. We just started this job and you are already making us enemies. I'm not trying to make anymore."

He slammed his locker shut and walked out. I didn't care. I was going to do it myself. When I left the district, I drove over to the hospital. As soon as I pulled up to the entrance, I saw a patrol car parked outside. I drove by the patrol car and saw Officer Morton sitting in the driver's seat. His partner wasn't in the car, so I assumed he was inside looking for the victims. Morton saw me ride by and he quickly got out of his patrol car. I looked in my rear view mirror and he was still watching me as I turned onto Broad Street. There was no way I could get into the hospital, so I had no other choice but to go home.

I got home and everything that went on was still on my mind. I worked out to try to focus my energy on something else, but it wasn't working. I could not stop thinking about everything that went on and how they were trying to cover things up. I continued working out until I forced myself to sleep. The next morning I woke up around 10:00 am to several missed calls and a voice message.

The call was made from a police department phone number and the message said, "Hello this message is for Officer Connor Mitchell. Officer Mitchell this is a message from Police Headquarters. You have been transferred to the 18th District, which is located at 55th and Pine Streets. You will be expected to arrive to the 18th District for your shift tonight and will report to Sergeant Lewis. If you have any questions please contact Police Headquarters." I literally dropped the phone when I heard the message. I sat there briefly, letting everything sink in. I picked up my phone and texted Reyes.

Me: *I just got transferred.*

Reyes: *Me too. They called me this morning.*

Me: *So you're going to the 18th too?*

Reyes: *Nope. She told me the 25th.*

Me: *Damn. They separated us. This had to be that damn Captain Nesmith.*

Reyes: *No this is on you. I told you to let it go man, now look at us.*

Me: *So this is my fault?*

Reyes: *Yea. You should have just left them alone. You were never going to win a battle with a captain.*

Me: No. *They aren't going to get away with this.*

Reyes: *It seems like they already did.*

Me: *We'll see*

Reyes: *SMH!*

After texting Reyes, I spent the rest of the day figuring out how I could get back at Nesmith. I had an idea and decided to type up the following letter:

To whom it may concern,

I am writing this letter to inform you of a disappointing form of corruption taking place in the Philadelphia Police Department. This corruption is mainly in the 35th District, but has currently extended to a high-ranking member of the department. To start, an investigation needs to be opened on Officer Morton, Officer Battles and Sergeant Wallace. They are unethical and have falsified a drug arrest report and an aggravated assault investigation. Officers Morton and Battles took credit for a drug arrest they did not make. They also assaulted another officer in their district when confronted about their lack of integrity. These actions were encouraged by the supervisor, Sergeant Wallace. Most recently, an aggravated assault took place outside the Dejavu bar and a bartender was brutally attacked by a current Police Recruit. The recruit's name is Adam Nesmith and he is the son of a Philadelphia Police Highway Patrol captain. This captain threatened the officers who were investigating the assault and he corrupted the entire investigation. As a result of refusing a bribe from Captain Nesmith, the two investigating officers were punished by being transferred to two separate districts. Please look into these matters. At this time, I do not know who can be trusted, so I will be having this letter delivered to multiple outlets. - Anonymous

I printed ten copies of the letter and placed them on a shelf in my closet. I had no idea who I was going to send the letters to, but I was determined to get my revenge on Captain Nesmith. I also wasn't going to let him run me out of my career, so I chose to use my relocation to the 18th District as a new start. I went into the 18th District that evening and met with Sergeant Lewis. During our first encounter, he didn't say much. I had no idea if he knew about the issues in the 35th District or if he was connected to Captain Nesmith in any way. He paired me up with two other rookies and our foot beat was in the area of 52nd and Spruce Streets. It was a hot muggy night in West Philly and I was getting accustomed to the streets and the atmosphere. While we were walking down 52nd Street, I saw two young men standing outside of a Sunoco gas station looking around. Moments later the men pulled handguns out from their waistbands and ran into the gas station. I could not see what was going on in the gas station, but I heard a woman screaming and gunshots. I began running towards the gas station and saw one of the gunman running out. My heart felt like it was beating out of my chest. I didn't know who he was, what happened inside the gas station or what was about to happen. The gunman ran directly towards my direction with the gun in his hand. Once he saw me, he stopped running and pointed the gun towards me. I heard a loud bang and saw a bright flash from the barrel of the gun. After the flash, I continued running. Between the utility belt and my heavy boots, I'm surprised I was able to keep up with him. I began chasing him down Spruce Street and my adrenaline was pumping. We ran down towards 49th Street and after each block, I closed the distance between us. I had no idea where the other rookies were, but I was gaining on the gunman. He suddenly turned and ran through a dark alleyway on 49th Street. I could not see much, only his silhouette as he ran away. He ran towards a tall metal gate that was around seven to eight feet tall. The gunman scaled the gate with ease, as if he had done it before. With my adrenaline pumping, I attempted to climb over the gate, but fell to the ground once I got over it. Once I hit the ground, equipment fell off my utility belt. There was no time to see what fell off so I got up and continued to chase the gunman through the alleyway. I gained distance on him and tackled him to the ground, causing his gun to slide across the concrete.

He reached for the gun but I was able to knock it away and under a trash dumpster. He began throwing punches at me, striking me several times in the face. I began punching back and got off a clean punch to his jaw, which stopped the attack. He curled up into a fetal position while blood poured from his mouth. I grabbed his left arm and bent it behind his back. He groaned as if he was in excruciating pain, but I could care less. I ordered him to put his right hand behind his back and he did so. The sound of his painful groans were like music to my ears, but the next sound I heard was much better.

It was the sound of cold steel tightening around his wrists as I handcuffed him. As soon as the gunman was cuffed, I realized we were alone in the alley and I had no idea what our exact location was. I saw the red and blue dome lights reflecting at the end of the alley. I had to get the attention of officers riding by, so I reached down to get my flashlight. As I felt around my utility belt, I noticed my light was missing. It must have dropped off when I fell over the gate. I was in an odd predicament because I had the prisoner cuffed and his gun was still under the dumpster. There was no way I was going to be able to walk back to the gate and look for my flashlight. I attempted to use the portable radio, but it appeared it might have been damaged during the fall. I was stuck with the prisoner and no immediate back up. Luckily, moments later an officer began shining their flashlight down the alley towards me. Suddenly several police officers ran over to my location. There were a lot of cheers and praise being given to me. I even heard someone say, “The rookie got his cherry popped.” I was all smiles until the ambulance pulled up to the location and paramedics began running towards me. My adrenaline began wearing off and I felt soreness and pain all over my body. The paramedics sat me down on the stretcher and began dabbing my face with a cloth. I could see blood on it, but I could not tell where it was coming from. For a moment, I was staring at the bloody cloth, but suddenly my eyes focused on the paramedic that was holding it. Her nametag read "Miller," but she introduced herself as Crystal. I had dozens of police officers congratulating me on a good arrest, but I was only focused on the rookies I was walking with. They came jogging up towards me.

"Damn you are on fast dude," one of them said. "We got the other guy in the store; he claimed your guy was the shooter."

"Did anyone get hit when he took that shot?"

"No, I don't think so. Good thing he has a bad aim because one of us would have surely gotten hit."

"You have a few lacerations on your face, a busted lip and abrasions on both your elbow and knee, but you will live" Crystal informed me. I smirked at her and she smiled back.

"Yo rook," it was the sound of Sergeant Lewis' voice coming towards me. I was excited, expecting praise from my superior officer. I heard Sergeant Lewis was a twenty-five year veteran of the force and had been involved in more than five police shootings, but they were just rumors.

"Where are you rookie?" Sergeant Lewis asked.

I had a look of confusion on my face because I didn't understand why he asked me that question.

"Where are you rookie? Go over the radio and give the dispatcher your location."

The last thing I remembered was running through the alley on 49th Street. I could not see the street signs from the alley. Sergeant Lewis had a look of frustration on his face.

"I don't know where I am at sir and I think the radio broke when I fell."

"Exactly" he replied, "If you were shot in the head, we wouldn't even know where to find your body. You are in a dark alley with a broken radio, no flashlight, no baton and luckily you had an extra pair of handcuffs."

He handed me an evidence bag with the equipment I dropped during the fall. The feeling of satisfaction I originally had quickly left and became a feeling of stupidity. I spent eight months in the police academy, where they always taught us to use the radio and always know our location. I did neither and on top of that, I dropped most of my equipment. I didn't think I could feel any worse. I was just shot at and Sergeant Lewis' only concern is every little thing I did wrong.

"Take a ride to the hospital and get checked out, I will deal with you later."

I replied, "Yes sir," although I wanted to tell him to go fuck himself.

I got into the back of the ambulance and heard Crystal's voice ask, "How are you doing?"

I sarcastically replied, "Well, it's my first day at this district and I already got shot at, got into a fight, got my ass ripped by my sergeant and now I'm on my way to the hospital. Not bad at all."

Crystal was doing paperwork in the passenger seat of the ambulance, while her partner drove to Hahnemann Hospital.

"Well I can't complain too much, at least I'm still alive."

Crystal looked back at me and smiled. I had so many thoughts running through my head about this night. I never expected my first day in the 18th District to be so action packed. I also wondered if Sergeant

Lewis was looking out for my safety or if he was looking for a reason to punish me. We arrived at the hospital, but my stay there was very brief. All the x rays came back negative for any fractures or broken bones. After the nurse cleaned and bandaged my wounds, I contacted the district to have someone pick me up. The doctor informed me that I would miss at least a week of work, to allow my wounds to completely heal.

After I was given my discharge paperwork, I was picked up by Officer Marcus Robinson who was a fifteen-year veteran of the force. Robinson told me that Sergeant Lewis was not very happy with me. I had a bad feeling about the work relationship I was going to have with Sergeant Lewis. They say first impressions are everything and I didn't make a good one with him. Especially because he probably already had a preconceived opinion about me. Robinson also responded to the robbery and was actually driving behind me while I was running after the suspect. I was grateful he was there because he said he was communicating with the dispatcher and letting her know my location. I thanked him and we talked the entire ride back to the district. He gave me very good advice and actually lifted my spirits about the entire night.

When we got back to the district, Sergeant Lewis was waiting for me. After everything I went through at my old district, I was determined to make things a lot better here. I got out of the car and immediately apologized to him.

"I just want to say I'm sorry sir, for being sloppy earlier."

"I can care less about your apology. I'm just here to let you know that Captain Nesmith gives his regards. You already made your first mistake today, if you keep this up I guarantee you won't make it here."

I knew it. I knew he had to be a part of all of this. "Listen Sergeant, I don't know what Captain Nesmith told you but I can guarantee it's not true. Nesmith is going down, so it would be in your best interest not to threaten me."

Sergeant Lewis didn't say another word to me and just walked away. I left to go home and I was convinced I needed to get out of this department. Once I got home, I began filling out applications online for other police departments. I had to get a Plan B in action, because who knows what else Captain Nesmith had up his sleeve. Once I finished filling out the applications, I walked over to the closet. I looked on the shelf and grabbed the stack of letters I typed. I had to send them out if I wanted to get rid of Captain Nesmith and his little crew. I left right out the house and drove to Police Headquarters and then to Internal Affairs.

I left copies of the letters in the mailboxes for the Police Commissioner, Deputy Commissioners, and the entire command staff at Internal Affairs. I was unsure if they were going to get the letters or do anything about it, but I planned to return every day with more letters until something was done. The entire time I was out of work with my injuries, I was still filling out applications and proceeding with the hiring processes with a few other police departments. After a week of not hearing anything about the letter, I copied them again and made a second round of deliveries. My next round of letters was going to go to media outlets and hopefully what Captain Nesmith and his followers were doing would go public. Another week passed and I received a phone call from a captain in Internal Affairs. They invited me down to their headquarters to make a formal statement about the bar incident and I did just that. I was happy to know they looked into the issues once they received my letter, because they tracked me down somehow. While I was walking into the interview room, I saw Reyes walking out of another one. He looked at me, smiled and gave me a reassuring head nod. I entered the interview room with an Internal Affairs Lieutenant and explained the entire situation with him. He was shocked that all this nonsense had gone on, but assured me it was finally coming to an end. After the interview, I texted Reyes:

Me: *I told you that Nesmith wouldn't get away with this.*

Officer Connor Mitchell left the Philadelphia Police Department and joined a police department in Bucks County, Pennsylvania. He is having a very productive career there and is very happy with his decision to relocate. Officer Angel Reyes is still currently serving with the Philadelphia Police Department. After receiving the letters, an Internal Affairs investigation was launched. As a result of that investigation, Captain Nesmith was forced to resign from the Department. Adam Nesmith was terminated as a recruit and charged with Aggravated Assault for the attack at that bar. Sergeant Wallace, Officer Morton and Officer Battles were all terminated from the Philadelphia Police Department. Sergeant Lewis was demoted back to a patrol officer, after the connection was made between Captain Nesmith and himself.

CHAPTER SIX

Officer Patrick McClain was a two-year veteran of the Philadelphia Police Department. He was born and raised in South Jersey. Patrick attended Rutgers University, where he obtained a Bachelor's Degree in Public Safety. After college, Patrick applied to become a Philadelphia police officer. Upon completing the police academy, Patrick served as a Patrol Officer in the 22nd District that covers the North Philadelphia section of Philadelphia. Like many people, Patrick had his share of financial hardships. Unlike most though, the badge gave him unique opportunities to pad his paycheck. Temptations that were too good to pass up, but would eventually cost him his career and even freedom.

This is Officer Patrick McClain's story...

SHAKEDOWN

I graduated the police academy in the spring of 2013. When I graduated, I walked a foot beat for six months with another rookie. I was twenty-two years old and my partner was only twenty-one. Walking the foot beat was fun, because we walked in the area of Temple University. We spent the entire summer assisting Temple University Police with out of control college parties and occasional robberies. The district was very busy, but we weren't too concerned. With all the shootings that were going on, we were having fun keeping the college scene quiet and safe. We had our whole careers ahead of us to chase around drug dealers and gang bangers, so we enjoyed our short time looking at beautiful college chicks. I will never forget the time we were walking by a huge party at a Fraternity House on 16th Street and a couple of the Frat Brothers invited us in. At first, everyone was looking at us funny and thought we were there to shut the party down. After the initial awkwardness went away, people began taking pictures with us and engaging in several conversations. We quickly became the highlight of the party and soon after, the highlight of almost all the Temple parties. The foot beat was a very fun time and it seemed like it flew by. In the winter of 2013, we were reassigned to normal patrol in the same district. All the rookies were split up and placed with veteran officers, who were assigned to train us.

My Training Officer was an eleven-year veteran named Jordan Daniels. Jordan started his career at twenty years old and seemed like he had a lot going for himself. As cool as he seemed, we didn't necessarily get off to a good start. I will never forget my first week of training. We were working the 4:00 pm to midnight shift, which was a very busy shift. Our first night working together he didn't even talk to me. He seemed bothered that I was riding with him and he didn't try to hide it either. As soon as the shift started, I grabbed my belongings and got into the passenger seat of the patrol car. He stood outside the car talking on the phone for about an hour. I sat in the car watching him, wishing I was back on my foot beat. After being on the phone, he walked back inside the district for about forty-five minutes. I was on my phone the entire time, while I waited for him to come back out. When he finally did, he got right into the patrol car and drove off. He didn't say a word; instead, he just turned the radio on. He drove to a local pizza shop and went in to eat. I went in to sit with him, but I was not hungry at the time so I just grabbed a soda.

He was on his phone the entire time we were in the pizza shop, so I never got the opportunity to spark up a conversation with him. By the time he was done eating and we left the pizza shop, we were three hours into our shift. As soon as we left, he pulled into the employee parking lot across from the district. He parked the car and turned the lights off. I had no idea what we were doing, so I just gazed out the window. After about thirty minutes, I looked over and saw Jordan sleeping. I could not believe this was happening. I was so excited coming out of the academy, after hearing so many stories about working the streets and this is what I got stuck with. I was very disappointed, but I knew there was nothing I could do. I learned very early that the Philadelphia Police Department was all about politics and everyone hated cops that snitched on other cops. So I just sat there looking around while he slept away the remainder of our shift. My stomach began growling, while he slept. I was so hungry and I didn't bring anything with me. I wanted to wake him up, to drive me to a store, but the last thing I wanted to do was get on the bad side of my training officer. So I just sat there starving, hoping he would wake up at some point. It seemed like this was his normal routine because he woke up just before the end of our shift. Even so, he didn't say one word to me. He just drove over to the district, packed his things up and left. I sat in the car starving for an entire shift, basically just as a lookout for him all evening. That was some bullshit.

When we walked back in the district, my old partner approached me and was very excited about his first day riding around.

Isn't this amazing?" he said. "We were ripping and running all shift. We even locked up some crazy guy that had a gun on him."

I looked at him and was so jealous because I had nothing to brag about, because my shift was the worst. "Well I'm glad you had fun because I didn't."

"Why not?"

"Because my lazy ass partner just parked up and went to sleep. We didn't do shit at all."

"Are you serious?"

"Dead serious."

"Well, maybe today was an off day for him. I'm sure he will be in full force tomorrow. Plus it's a Friday night, so it will be too much action going on to be sleeping."

Maybe he was right and tomorrow will be a great day.

That night a bunch of training officers told the rookies to meet up at the FOP Lodge 5 for some drinks. I was amazed that they were going to take us out on our first day. This was going to be a positive ending to a very bad day. We went straight to Lodge 5 after work and had a good time. There was music playing and drinks flowing all night. Jordan showed up, but didn't even acknowledge that I was in the room. The entire time he was walking around mingling with other officers and never said a word to me. When the night was over, one of the veteran officers got on the microphone and made an announcement.

He said, "I'd like to thank everyone for coming out tonight to celebrate the rookies first day off their foot beats. To all the rookies, take a look around at all these veteran officers and make sure you learn from them. This is not an easy job to do, but we all signed up for it. Also, look at the food and beer these veterans ate and drank tonight. They are very thankful because sincc tonight is rookie night, guess who the bill for all this goes to? So, I suggest all you rookies gather up and figure out how you all are going to pay this bill. Have a good night everyone."

The whole room began to cheer and all the rookies looked around in disappointment. It was all a complete hazing technique. They brought us all here just to screw us over at the end of the night. I had a feeling all of it was too good to be true. For someone who wasn't even being acknowledged by his training officer, I felt as if I should have been exempt from this rookie hazing.

I began walking towards the exit, when one of the veteran officers yelled, "someone's rookie is trying to leave."

Everyone in the building began booing me and a few officers pulled me away from the door. The next thing I saw was Jordan walking up towards the DJ booth and grabbing the microphone.

He got everyone's attention and stated, "Since this little bitch tried to sneak out, hand him the bill. He's in charge of collecting all of the rookies' money."

Looking in my direction, he gave me two middle fingers and stepped down from the DJ booth. Once again, cheers and laughter roared the building. So great, he doesn't even acknowledge me but decided to disrespect me in front of everyone. One of the servers walked over to me and handed me the night's bill, which was well over five thousand dollars. I walked around the room trying to collect money from the other new officers, while they tried to nickel and dime me. I think the most money someone gave me was a hundred dollars and I was stuck with thirty five hundred dollars remaining on the bill. With anger boiling in my veins, I went up to the DJ booth and grabbed the microphone.

"Ok assholes, ya'll need to pay up. I only got fifteen hundred dollars from all of you and that didn't even cover half the bill."

No later than when I spoke my last word, people began walking out like nothing happened.

"Well fuck all of ya'll motherfuckers," I yelled.

I walked towards the server and she just smiled.

"They get someone every year," she said while she laughed.

"What a wonderful way to start a career."

I handed her the cash I collected and my credit card to pay the remainder of the bill. After leaving Lodge 5, I was ready to call my sergeant and ask not to work with Jordan ever again. He really didn't make a good first impression on me and after that little stunt at Lodge 5, I wanted no parts of him. I decided not to make the call at that moment and went home to sleep on the decision.

The next day I woke up barely in time for work. When I got there, I didn't say a word to Jordan. That really didn't matter because it's not like he actually talked to me anyway. After roll call, he looked at me and got right into the patrol car. I got into the patrol car too, hoping it would be an eventful night. Once Jordan began driving, it seemed like he was following the same routine as the night before. I could not believe we were doing this again. He headed to the same pizza shop to get his dinner and this time I didn't even go in with him. I just waited in the car. He spent two hours in the pizza shop while tons of calls were being dispatched over the radio. There were robberies, a fight at a house party and a ton of domestic disturbances going on.

It was so busy and we were doing nothing but sitting around. I was not learning anything at all. Jordan finally came out from the shop and drove to the same parking lot from the night before. Within five minutes of parking the car, he was knocked out cold again. I began snapping pictures of him sleeping on my cell phone. My intention was to send the picture to the sergeant, so I could be partnered up with someone else. I started to text the picture to the sergeant when I saw some headlights pulling into the parking lot. I quickly turned to Jordan and hit him in the chest, which woke him up. As soon as I did, the car pulled up and it was our Chief Inspector. If he would have saw Jordan sleeping, Jordan would have definitely been suspended. The Chief inspector stopped to tell us about a group of people standing in front of a house on Gratz Street. He believed the people may have been dealing drugs and wanted us to check them out. Once he said that, I was excited because this was going to be my first official job.

"Come on rook" Jordan said. "It's time to pop your cherry."

Jordan drove over to Gratz Street. As we pulled onto the block, I could see a group of young dudes standing in front of a house on the left side of the street. The house was towards the middle of the block. Once we pulled up to the group, they all began running. There had to be about seven or eight of them running away in different directions. I hopped out the car and chased one of the dudes. I will never forget him because he was wearing these bright orange Nike sneakers, which caught my attention and made me focus on him. I focused on those bright sneakers as he ran up Gratz Street beside one of the other dudes. Initially it appeared as if he was going to continue running on Gratz Street, but he made a quick maneuver and took off up Berks Street. By the time I turned the corner, he was almost a full block ahead of me.

I swear he had speed like a cheetah. Those bright sneakers seemed very far the more I ran. My heart was racing; I heard the clanking of the handcuffs on my duty belt and felt the hard cement under my boots. My boots seemed to be getting heavier the more I ran. Suddenly I saw my suspect turn the corner onto Woodstock Street. I continued chasing him, but once I turned onto Woodstock Street he was nowhere in sight. I walked up Woodstock Street checking between parked cars, thinking he was hiding, but there was no sign of him. I walked up to Norris Street and it was clear that he was long gone. I was breathing heavily and my uniform was soaked with sweat. I had a very long and embarrassing walk back to Gratz Street. I couldn't believe I got smoked on my first foot chase. I wanted to come back and impress Jordan with an arrest, but that wasn't happening. As I walked back to Gratz Street, I heard laughter and heckling from neighbors who saw me get outran. I'm sure they enjoyed every second of the chase. When I walked around the corner and saw Jordan, he burst out laughing.

"Let me guess, you didn't catch him?" he asked.

"Ha ha ha. You wouldn't have caught him either."

"You damn right I wouldn't have caught him, because I wouldn't have chased him in the first place."

"Yea yea, whatever," I yelled and began walking away.

"Hey rook, what were you chasing him for?"

"What? What do you mean what was I chasing him for?"

"Did I stutter or something? I asked you what the hell were you chasing that guy for?" he asked in a very demanding voice.

"I was chasing him because he ran. All of them ran."

"Your job is to fight crime. Tell me what crime they committed."

"They ran from the police."

"Is running a crime?"

I didn't even respond to his question. I stood there with a blank stare on my face, because obviously Jordan thought I did something wrong. Jordan walked over to me and shoved a hard object in my chest. I grabbed the object, which was a small lock box. I opened the box to reveal its contents. A silver revolver, bullets and what appeared to be a few bundles of heroin were inside to box.

Jordan came back up to me and said, "Rule number one on the streets is ninety-nine percent of the time they run because they want you to chase them. They want you to chase them because it gets you away from what they don't want you to find. Plus, they know that just running from the cops isn't a crime and only young and dumb cops chase them. Let this be a lesson learned rook."

Jordan walked up to the house the group was standing in front of and began looking around. I didn't understand what he was looking for. He already found the lock box, there couldn't possibly be anything else to find. Suddenly I saw him pushing on the door and windows. He found one window that he was able to force open.

He began shining his flashlight inside and yelled out "Got it." Jordan reached inside the window and grabbed a book bag. He peeked in the bag and began walking back towards the patrol car.

He put the bag in the trunk and said, "Come on rook, let's go." I got into the car and he drove back to the district.

Once we got back to the district, Jordan told me to go inside and put the items in the lock box into evidence.

"This is one of the parts of the job that sucks rook. You have to do a bunch of paperwork and you don't even have an arrest. It is a complete waste of time, but you have to learn how to do the paperwork. As I walked inside, I looked back and saw Jordan drive over towards his personal car. I went inside the district to begin the paperwork for the evidence and minutes later Jordan walked in.

"So what happens to this stuff?"

"Absolutely nothing. You put them into evidence and they just sit there. After a certain amount of years, it gets destroyed by the department. The main thing is you got if off the streets."

"Oh ok. So where's the rest of the stuff?"

"What stuff?"

"The bag you grabbed out the window, don't you want me to put that with this stuff?"

"Don't worry about that stuff. It was a bag full of crap. I threw it out."

As soon as he said that, he walked away and got on his phone. I didn't think anything of it and continued typing the property receipts for the evidence inside the lock box. This process took longer than I expected because the forms had to be completed using a typewriter and I had to start over from scratch every time I made a mistake. It was hard to believe such a large department was so behind on technology in 2013. Other officers were walking by and laughing because they saw the pile of wrong property receipts sitting next to me. After an entire hour of failed attempts, I finally got the property receipt done correctly. I definitely agreed with Jordan that this was a complete waste of time.

Our sergeant approached me and stated, "McClain, I got a call from the Chief Inspector and he said you two did a good job clearing out that block tonight."

"Thanks sir."

A very gratifying feeling came over me. I had a complete change of feelings about Jordan. I no longer felt the need to request a different training officer. The rest of the evening went smooth and I could tell things were getting off to a better start between us.

The next evening I came into work things started out great. After roll call, Jordan seemed excited to go out and work. He even asked me what I felt like doing, which was any and everything. I was still in learning mode, so I didn't care what we did. I was certain that we were going to head to the pizza shop, but we didn't. We patrolled the district and I got the opportunity to learn the streets and some of the high crime areas in North Philly. During our patrol, a radio call was dispatched for a suspicious male at 24th and Berks Street. A neighbor claimed the male was possibly selling drugs in the area. The only description the neighbor provided was a light-skinned black male wearing a blue hoodie and grey sweatpants. The information we received also said the male might be using a white Mercury Grand Marquis to make transactions. We entered the area and observed a male fitting that description walking down 24th Street. We ended up stopping the male to speak to him. He ended up not having anything on him and denied owning the Grand Marquis or being near it. Jordan walked over to the Grand Marquis and starting looking through it. The car was unlocked and since the male didn't claim ownership, Jordan began going through it. Jordan popped open the hood, trunk and gas lid on the Grand Marquis. As soon as he did this, he looked over to towards us and smiled. He began putting something in his pocket and then walked towards us.

He looked at the suspect and asked, "So is this your car?"

"Nope I don't have a car. I catch Septa."

"So I'm guessing this isn't you're heroin too?" Jordan asked. When he asked the question, he held up a bundle pack of heroin and pushed it in the male's face.

"Oh hell no. I don't know whose shit that is."

"Good answer. Now get off my block because next time I catch you out here, you're getting locked up" Jordan said calmly.

The suspect walked off very fast and went into a house at the end of the block.

Jordan said, "Come on rook, let's go."

We got into the car and Jordan held up the bundle. "So do you want the honors of going back to the district and logging this into evidence?" he asked while laughing.

"Honestly I don't feel like doing all that paperwork again."

Jordan laughed and said, "Now you're learning rook. Work smarter, not harder."

He put the bundle in his pocket and we continued working throughout the night. Things went smooth again on this night. We handled a few calls such as domestics and medical emergencies, but that was about it. These calls were easy, they just weren't exciting. I knew I gravitated more towards the high profile jobs. I wanted the robberies, shootings and kidnappings. Plus, I saw how the guys who made a lot of arrests got praise and special treatment from the supervisors. Jordan was different though; he didn't care about any of those things and didn't want me focusing on them either.

After our shift, Jordan invited me over to his house for a drink. I was shocked when he did this, but was happy because our bond was getting tighter. I followed behind Jordan, who was driving his brand new Chevy Camaro and I could barely keep up in my old Ford

Explorer. I didn't know this but Jordan lived in Cheltenham, Pennsylvania which was just minutes outside Philadelphia. His house was amazing. Three stories, three-car garage and the yard was huge. My mouth dropped to the floor when we pulled up. In his driveway was a new Mercedes Benz CLS550 that was glimmering from the reflection of the moon. It was white with white rims. I could not believe what I was seeing and I got excited because there was a possibility that one day this could be me. We walked inside his home and it was gorgeous. It looked like something out of a magazine and it left me speechless. Coming from South Jersey, I had to move into a little apartment off Rhawn Street, which was nothing impressive. Jordan introduced me to his wife Sarah, who was up watching some type of home makeover show on television. She was a very beautiful woman and seemed very nice. He was one lucky guy. Jordan started off by showing me pictures of his four children, who were absolutely adorable.

"This is who I do it for," he said. "I wanted to make sure they were going to get the best everything from education to lifestyle. I will do anything necessary to maintain this lifestyle for my family."

I looked at him and smirked. "Man honestly it seems like you have it all."

He poured us some rum and coke and replied, "Yea I do. But it's not about getting it, it's about keeping it. I'm going on my twelfth year with the city and I was just like you when I came out the academy. I saw when you were looking at those officers at the end of the shift that were getting their ass kissed by the sergeant. Your time will come."

"Yea I just want to do a good job and get recognition for my hard work."

Jordan got up and went into a closet. He pulled out what appeared to be a binder and slammed it in front of me. I opened the binder and there were tons of awards, certificates and commendations he received on the job. It was astonishing and I was proud of him for obtaining these accomplishments. Jordan chugged down his drink and poured himself another.

"All of those mean nothing at the end of the day" he said. "Do you know how many times I took the test to become a sergeant? Do you know how many times I applied for Swat? For the K-9 Unit? For anything in this damn job?" he asked. "You will see that hard work does not always pay off in the department, it's all politics. It's all about who you know and whose ass you're willing to kiss to get where you want. I refuse to belittle myself to get somewhere in this department. Instead, I just do what I want. So you need to think about what kind of career you want to have. You are either going to be someone who kisses ass or someone who takes what he wants."

I had no idea where any of this was coming from but obviously I wanted the lifestyle Jordan had, so I was definitely going to follow his advice.

We stayed up all night, into the morning, drinking and talking. I learned a lot about Jordan and he learned a lot about me. I didn't have much going on for myself and I definitely didn't have any connections in the department. He convinced me to look out for my own personal interests and not get caught up trying to get approval from anyone else. We went on to have some good times at work. We made many arrests and grew closer. I felt that Jordan always had my back and I definitely had his. The year 2014 came quick and we rolled right into the spring.

The weather was becoming nicer and crime seemed to be rising. We got so many calls about drugs and gang related activities, it was getting out of control. Jordan and I were making arrests left and right. During this time, the Police Commissioner implemented a permanent 6:00 pm to 2:00 am shift, which Jordan and I volunteered for immediately. We figured we would see more action on this shift and it worked out for him when he had to get his children from school. Everything was falling into place and seemed perfect. During the spring, my old Ford was giving me problems and I was late to work a few times. I ended up being written up by my supervisor for excessive lateness. On top of that, the rent in my apartment went up and I was falling behind on my student loans. I kept these issues to myself but Jordan noticed a change in my behavior, due to stress. It was sometime in April, when I finally told Jordan everything that was going on.

We were patrolling and I looked at him and said, “Man, I am stressed out. I’m having financial issues and I need to find a new car.”

Jordan immediately pulled over and asked, “How much money would help you with these financial issues?”

I thought about it and replied, “At least eight or nine thousand just to get me above water. But where the hell am I going to find that type of money?”

He drove back to the District and went inside the building. I waited in the car for about an hour before he came back out. Jordan got back into the car and handed me an envelope. I opened the envelope and inside was a check made out to me, from him. The check was made out for ten thousand dollars.

I dropped the envelope. “Man, I can’t take this from you. I couldn’t take this type of money from your family and I wouldn’t even know how to pay you back in time.”

I was flustered because it totally caught me off guard. That was a whole lot of money and it would unquestionably benefit me a lot.

Jordan looked at me and said, "Listen take it and get yourself together, don't worry about paying me back right now. By the way, you are family now."

"Where the hell did you get this type of money."

"My savings. Stashing money away over the years for emergencies. This seems like an emergency."

I couldn't help but be in a great mood all night. I swear meeting Jordan was the best thing that ever happened to me.

The next day, I woke up and went straight to the bank to deposit the check. It was time to pay off all my debt and stop living paycheck to paycheck. Jordan drove me to the bank, so there wouldn't be a hold to verify the funds. We rode in his Mercedes and it was very nice. That car was amazing and luxurious. After leaving the bank, he went over to the Ford dealership with me to check on the status of my Explorer, which had been in the repair shop for weeks. We got to the dealership and I spoke to the Service Manager. He told me I was looking at roughly five thousand dollars in repairs to get my Explorer back to good condition and that wouldn't even guarantee it would run consistently.

Jordan burst out laughing and said, "You better not even waste your time or money on that junk. That Explorer has over a hundred and eighty five thousand miles on it; it is probably not even worth five grand. What you need to is use that money as a down payment and get that right there."

I looked over at Jordan and saw him pointing in the direction of the new cars. He walked over and stood next to a brand new Ford Mustang.

"This is what you need right here. This is a beauty."

I definitely agreed, but I didn't know if I would be able to afford a fifty thousand dollar car.

"You only live once, so make sure you live your life. You're a young, single man with no kids so why the hell are you worried about a big clunky SUV. Come over to the coupe life with me" Jordan said.

He was very convincing and talked me into getting the Mustang. It was truly a beauty. All black everything from the exterior to the interior leather seats. I got into my brand new Mustang and I literally felt that my life was going so well because of Jordan. I was the new owner of a 2015 Ford Mustang Shelby GT500. When we left, you know I had to show off. We stopped by Jordan's house so he could switch into his Camaro and we hit the streets. From Roosevelt Boulevard, to 1-95, to Broad Street, we were out. Hitting speeds over a hundred and twenty miles per hour, with the adrenaline flowing through my body. I was in love with my new car. I followed Jordan down to South Street, where he did some shopping. While on South Street, I met a very nice woman. Her name was Emma and she was drop dead gorgeous. She had the prettiest blue eyes, long red hair and the cutest freckles on her face. She was with a friend and they were visiting from Jersey. Immediately we hit it off because we had our little Jersey connection. We talked for a while and eventually exchanged numbers. This felt like the best day in the world and I felt like things were definitely turning around for me. After Jordan was done shopping, we went over to his house to hang out. We sat in his yard smoking cigars and talking about finances.

"Listen Pat, everything isn't going to be easy, but you have to want it."

"What do you mean?"

"You will see soon enough, but if you roll with me, you have to be loyal no matter what."

"Listen Jordan, I owe you so much and I will never cross you, I promise you that."

After the conversation, we sat around relaxing until it was time to go to work.

The shift went smooth. We pretty much did what we wanted when we got to work because we were productive. Since the weather was nice, we were able to see all the locations the drug dealers were hanging out at. We also got to know which houses were being used as party houses and which ones were stash spots. On this night, Jordan felt like hitting one of the stash spots, which was located at 22nd and Diamond Streets. It was almost midnight and there was the usual foot traffic that goes on in North Philly. We parked on the corner of 22nd Street and watched as a few people went in and out a rundown house on Diamond Street. The house looked abandoned and there were wooden boards over almost every window. They appeared to have a lookout man, who was sitting on the step and never really moved. He was going to be the first person we had to worry about because he would be able to see us driving up the block.

"Let's just walk up to the house and surprise the guy?" I suggested.

Jordan agreed and that's exactly what we did. We quietly got out the patrol car and crept up on the opposite side of the street. We were crouched down behind parked cars, so he definitely didn't see us approaching. As soon as we got close enough we jumped out on him. He was so startled, he actually reached down towards his waistband. Jordan and I drew our guns and I yelled, "Police. Don't move!" He froze in place and slowly put his hands in the air. I gripped him up and placed him under arrest. After the arrest, we searched him and found a 9mm Ruger handgun tucked in the front of his waistband. The gun was fully loaded and I'm sure he intended on using it. Jordan told me to stand outside with the suspect, as he checked the house. I cleared the Ruger and tucked it in my pocket.

I looked at the suspect and asked him, "Do you live here?"

"Naw, my homie do."

"Who's your homie? What's his name?"

"His name is Doughboy."

I chuckled because I knew his friend didn't live at the home. It never fails, every time I ask someone about their friend they always tell me someone's nickname.

Jordan opened the door and announced, "Police! If anyone's in here you need to come out now." I was outside and I could hear what sounded like multiple people scrambling around inside. Jordan waited briefly before entering. He checked the interior of the home and came back outside. When he came back out, he walked up the street to get the patrol car. He pulled up; I put the suspect in the rear of the car and saw Jordan going in the trunk. He gave me an evidence bag for the gun and he took an empty black duffel bag out the trunk.

"I'll be right back," he mumbled and walked into the stash house.

After about fifteen minutes, Jordan came back out with the duffel bag and placed it in the trunk. When he came out the duffel bag appeared to be full. We drove back to the district, processed the suspect and placed the gun into evidence. I sat inside doing the paperwork and Jordan said he was going to get us some food. He came back an hour later with two cheesesteaks and I still wasn't done the paperwork.

"Damn rook, you type like an old lady," he said and started laughing.

I looked at him and started laughing. "Well its lunch time, so I'm taking a break," I said and began eating my cheesesteak.

"I don't blame you. When you're done, I want to show you something," Jordan said as he gave me a serious look.

I nodded my head and continued eating.

After I finished the arrest paperwork, I met Jordan outside in the district parking lot. We walked to the trunk of our patrol car and he opened it. As the trunk opened, the first thing I saw was the duffel bag.

"Open it," said Jordan. I slowly unzipped the bag and couldn't believe what was inside. Inside the bag was a lot of cash and what appeared to be two kilos of heroin. I immediately closed the bag and looked around to make sure no one was watching us.

"What the hell is this?"

"This is what I found in the house. Whoever it belonged to ran out and I wasn't going to leave it in the house for them to come back and get it."

"Well what are we going to do with it?"

He gave me a stern look and said, "That's totally up to you. You can either take it inside and type up a property receipt for all of it or get rid of it."

"Man, I'm definitely not going in there typing up no damn receipts for all this shit, so I guess we just get rid of it."

Jordan smiled and said, "Good answer."

Initially I didn't think anything of it, so I didn't ask any questions. We got in the car and Jordan drove over to his Camaro. He put the duffel bag in the trunk of the Camaro and we went back inside the district. Once we walked inside, we ran into our sergeant.

"Daniels, McClain, come here," the sergeant said.

I looked over at Jordan, because I knew we were done. I just knew the sergeant was going to ask us about the duffel bag. I was so nervous and I felt my stomach drop down to my balls.

Jordan turned around and stated, "Yes Sarge."

"Good job today, I heard you guys got a gun off the street tonight," the sergeant said.

"Yup, we got it off some little punk earlier," I said.

The sergeant shook our hands and said, "You guys can cut out early, as soon as you get done your paperwork. You did your job tonight."

We thanked the sergeant and got to leave work early. I was happy because we were off for the next two days. Jordan and I planned to link up during our days off. When we were leaving work, I headed down to Broad Street to go home. I stopped at a red light when I got to Allegheny Avenue and I suddenly heard the revving of an engine next to me. I looked over and saw Jordan next to me, ready to race. I gripped the steering wheel and took off as soon as the light turned green. We were going Mach-1 down Broad Street and the rush was amazing. By the time we got to the area of Broad and Hunting Park, I could see the headlights of the Camaro in my side mirror. I turned off, got on Roosevelt Boulevard and headed home.

The next day I woke up, I received a call from Emma. She wanted to see me, so we decided to meet up for lunch. I met her downtown and we walked down to Love Park. We were talking and getting to know each other. After our little walk, we went over to Del Frisco's restaurant. While we were eating, I got a text from Jordan.

Jordan: *Yo wyd?*

Me: *Nothin much. I'm downtown with the girl I met down South Street.*

Jordan: *What are ya'll doing?*

Me: *Having lunch at Del Friscos. Wyd?*

Jordan: *Nothing much. I need to link up with you real quick.*

Me: Ok. *Meet us down here.*

Jordan: *I will bring wifey with me. We're on our way.*

Me: *Ok. No problem.*

I told Emma that Jordan and his wife were coming down to join us. She was excited to meet them because I told her all about them during our walk. When they got there, we had a great time. We sat at the bar, had drinks and many laughs. During the conversations, Jordan pulled me to the side. We walked to a quieter area of the restaurant and left the women to get to know each other better.

"I got something for you," Jordan said.

"What is it?"

He handed me an envelope that felt thick. I opened the envelope and saw a ton of cash inside. I closed it and looked around to make sure no one saw it.

"What the hell is this?" I asked curiously.

"That's half the money from the duffel bag. I got rid of the drugs, now I'm getting rid of the cash."

"Man, I can't take this money."

"Listen, either you take it, we throw it in the trash with the drugs or we turn it in as evidence and the state gets it."

In my head, he made a valid point and I guess the best decision to make would be to keep it. Plus, I definitely needed the money. I looked at him and gave him a big hug. I could use this money to pay off my student loans and even start repaying Jordan for the money he loaned me. We returned to our women and I ordered more drinks for everyone. This was just the beginning of a great friendship between all of us. Over the next few months, Emma and I became close and started dating. She became a big part of my life and I cared about her a whole lot. I needed someone special to give my heart to and she was the one for me.

At work, things were going great. Hitting stash houses throughout the district became a common occurrence for us. Some nights we would even mask up before we kicked in doors, which scared the shit of many of the drug dealers. They probably thought we were a rival gang or the feds when they saw us coming in. We began coming home with five to ten thousand dollars a month. Life was very good and things were looking up. I was able to pay off all my debt and pay Jordan back the money he let me borrow. I even put a down payment on a nice big house in the Northeast section of Philadelphia. Things slowly began to change in the winter of 2014. During this time, we had already hit all the stash houses and things were slowing up. This was a problem because obviously Jordan and I were living beyond our means and paychecks. We had lifestyles we needed to support and we had to find a way how. Jordan was becoming obsessed, which made him sloppy. People in the neighborhood would see him kicking in doors to abandoned houses and seeing the frustration on his face when he would come out empty handed. He would forget to mask up, so the dealers knew exactly who he was. I tried to get him back on track, but he was a very determined man.

After a few weeks of the same unproductive routine, we received roll call information about possible drugs sales out of a home on Willington Street. The building was apparently an off-site apartment for a few Temple University students. A confidential informant gave one of our detectives information that there are a lot of drugs in that house. As soon as we broke from roll call, Jordan and I drove down to the block. No one was outside the building, so I chose to get a closer look. The building definitely wasn't abandoned and you could tell students were inside. There was a big Temple University sticker in the window. Something didn't feel right about this house. There was no crime besides a little tip from someone we didn't even know. I went back to the car and told Jordan this wasn't one of the easy jobs. I told him we needed to leave and just go patrol. The next thing I heard was "fuck this shit." Jordan stormed out the car, grabbed his duffel bag from the trunk and went up to the house. Our patrol car was still parked in the middle of the street. Jordan knocked on the door and someone answered. As soon as the door began opening, Jordan pushed it in, which knocked the person who opened the door to the ground. We went into the home and sure enough, there were five students sitting around a table packaging up a ton of drugs. There was marijuana, cocaine, ecstasy and a ton of cash sitting on the table. We ordered all the students to kneel against the wall and one person in particular was doing most of the talking.

"Officers please, I can explain. We were just trying to make some money to pay for our tuition."

Jordan walked over to him and said, "Well maybe ya'll should have gotten real jobs. You are all looking at felony charges. I need all of your names."

He began gathering their information and told me to start collecting all the evidence.

The guy began crying and begged, "Please officers, take everything. Take it all, just give us a break."

"You heard the man, take it all," Jordan said, as he looked at me smiling.

After I gathered all the stuff, I announced, "Now no one move until we come back in." Jordan and I walked out the house and drove off. As we drove off, I had a weird feeling in my gut. Our actions were not sitting right with me, but I didn't want to piss Jordan off so I kept my opinion to myself. I could not second-guess the man that helped me out when I was at my lowest point. I promised him I would be loyal and I planned to do just that. Jordan put the duffel bag in his trunk and we continued our normal patrol for the night. He was full of energy for the remainder of the night. I continued to check the radio to see if the dealers on Willington Street would make a report, but nothing came out for their address. After our shift, I called Emma and spent the rest of the night in Jersey with her. I needed something to take my mind off everything we did that night and Emma was the perfect distraction.

Work became very confusing for me after what we did the night before. It was clear that Jordan and I were on two different pages. I had no problem when we were taking stuff from stash spots, that would just sit around in the evidence room, but it was different actually robbing someone in their own home. What I thought was a one-time thing became a very bad habit. What started out as hitting stash houses, turned into just taking whatever we could off low and high level drug dealers. We began building a reputation in the streets as the "shakedown cops." Dealers used to give their goods right up, when we made contact with them. As time passed, getting what we wanted became easier and we were also putting up good numbers when it came to work activity.

Although other officers were getting accolades from the department, Jordan and I were living luxurious lives. That was the only accolade I needed. I was a young broke kid from jersey that was now able to buy whatever I wanted. In the spring of 2015, I bought a Range Rover and got some renovations done to my house. Sometimes I would wake up and just go shopping as a hobby. We were making so much extra money, I decided to live a lavish lifestyle. I had all the finer things in life, I ate at the finest restaurants in the city and I had one of the finest women in the world. Emma moved in with me in May of 2015 and we were actually expecting our first child. Emma never questioned anything I did and I never mentioned it to her. The only thing we discussed was our future together. I planned to propose to her in September and she had no idea. It would seem all the plans I had for the future would change that summer.

It was a cool July night and there was a full moon. The moon was so bright it lit up the streets of North Philly like a spotlight. Jordan and I left roll call and went to hit the streets. It was an active night and we were ripping and running all night. Everything began to quiet down around half past midnight. We were patrolling, when we rode pass Bouvier Street. As we drove pass Bouvier, I looked down the street and observed a black sedan stopped in the middle of the block. There was someone wearing a black hoodie standing outside the driver's door of the sedan. Jordan and I parked up and crept up the block, just as we did the last time. As we crept up, I saw that the sedan was stopped directly in front of a drug house that we had hit before. We jumped out on them and caught them by surprise. I gripped up the dude in the hoodie and Jordan focused on the driver of the car.

"Put your hands on the car," I ordered the dude in the hoodie. I frisked him and felt a large bulge in his right front pocket.

"What the hell is that?" I asked.

"Money"

"Why do you have all that money on you out here in a known drug area?"

"It's my income tax money."

I burst out laughing and said, "Income tax money in July? Must be nice."

"I don't get what's so funny."

"You're funny, you piece of shit."

Jordan overheard this conversation and began questioning the driver of the car. "Ok, so he has the money, which means you must have something he wants to buy," Jordan said to the driver.

"Umm, officer is there something wrong? Did I commit a crime?" the driver asked.

Jordan seemed aggravated and stated, "Let's see, you're a white boy on a North Philly drug block and you look a little old to be a Temple Student. So you must be here for something drug related. So yes, you are committing a crime."

"But officer-" the driver began talking and Jordan cut him off.

"What the fuck do you have in that bag back there?" Jordan asked, as he was shining his flashlight into the back seat area of the car.

"Nothing officer, that's just my bag. Am I free to go?"

Jordan opened the rear door and removed the bag from the back seat. He opened the bag and dumped it on top the car. Three kilos of heroin fell out the bag and onto the car.

Jordan put one of the kilos in the driver's face and asked him "what's this?"

"I can explain."

"Oh, I don't think there is much to explain."

"No there is."

"Do you want to go to jail or do you want to go home?"

"I want to go home."

Jordan grabbed the remainder of the kilos and placed them all in the bag. He threw the bag over his shoulder, looked at the driver and said, "Well if you want to go home, you better start driving before a change my mind and lock you up."

The driver of the sedan took off as soon as Jordan finished his statement. I took the money from the dude I had stopped and said, "I suggest you get out of here too." He ran off and we walked back to our patrol car. I handed the money to Jordan and he put it in the bag. Jordan dropped me off at the district and drove over to his Camaro, as he usually did. I went inside the district and began talking to other officers that were inside.

As I stood inside, I heard the door swing open behind me. I turned around and saw at least six people march into the district with my sergeant. These people were wearing full tactical gear and carrying rifles.

"That's him right there, Sergeant," a distant voice said, as the men marched in.

I looked and suddenly I saw a figure walk to the front of the crowd. My mouth dropped to the floor and I felt so heavy. The person who spoke walked towards me, with fire in his eyes. IT WAS THE DRIVER. The driver that we just stole the drugs from marched right into the district and was now wearing a jacket that displayed a "Federal Agent" and "ATF" patch. I didn't fully understand exactly what was taking place, but I knew I was in big trouble. Two of the people from the group grabbed me and I tried pushing them off. I was out numbered and out powered. They placed me under arrest while I was in full uniform. This was so embarrassing. All the other officers from the district were standing around in shock and whispering.

"You really thought you would get away with doing this type of stuff?" he asked. I refused to answer his question and just looked right into his eyes with a devilish glare.

"Well, congratulations," he said. "I'm special agent Ryan Walton with the ATF and you just robbed me ten minutes ago.

My sergeant walked over and asked, "Is all this stuff true Pat?"

I didn't answer him either; I just hung my head in disappointment.

"Yes it's absolutely true, Sergeant," Agent Walton said. "This officer is a thief and his partner is one of the biggest drug dealers in the city."

When I heard this, I couldn't believe it. What the hell did he mean when he said Jordan was one of the biggest drug dealers in the city?

"What do you mean?" I asked with a very confused look on my face.

"Oh, now you can talk? Well from the dumb look on your face, I guess your partner didn't tell you he was selling the drugs you two were stealing," Agent Walton said.

I felt betrayed and hurt. Jordan lied to me this entire time. He always told me he trashed the drugs we took. I had no idea he was selling the drugs. Seconds later, other agents escorted Jordan in the district in handcuffs. He held his head down the entire time and avoided looking at me. Word travelled quickly and it seemed like all the officers came back to the district just to see what was going on. Jordan and I were escorted out the district and placed in the back of one of the agent's vehicles. We were being transported to the processing center and that was the end of my law enforcement career.

One of Officer Daniels and Mitchell's victims was a Federal Informant. He tipped of the ATF of two officers in North Philly that were stealing drugs and reselling them. The

ATF, FBI and the Philadelphia Police Internal Affairs Bureau launched an investigation on the officers in 2014. The investigation led to the setup of a false drug sale with the informant, which would attract the attention of the officers. After the robbery, Jordan Daniels was followed and the Federal Agents obtained footage of him placing the stolen goods into the trunk of his Camaro. Officer Patrick McClain was arrested and charged with multiple counts of corruption, theft and extortion. Officer Jordan Daniels was arrested and also charged with multiple counts of corruption, theft and extortion, along with distributing heroin, cocaine, ecstasy and marijuana. Both officers were terminated from the Philadelphia Police Department. Patrick McClain was found guilty and sentenced to serve fifteen years in Federal Prison. Jordan Daniels was found guilty and sentenced to serve thirty years in Federal Prison. During the investigation, agents linked the drug sales to the assets of both officers. Due to Asset Forfeiture, their houses, cars and other assets, believed to be purchased with drug money, were seized. Their families were literally left with nothing.

CHAPTER SEVEN

Officer Christopher Chung was a thirteen-year veteran of the Philadelphia Police Department. He grew up in the Olney section of the city. He is a father of two boys and is currently engaged to his longtime girlfriend. Growing up, Christopher truly admired his own father, who used to be a Philadelphia police officer as well. At a very young age, he had already made the decision to follow in his father's footsteps and serve his city. After high school, Christopher obtained his Bachelor's Degree in Criminal Justice from West Chester University and applied to become a Philadelphia police officer. He completed the police academy and served his duties in the 3rd District, which covered parts of South Philadelphia. He had a proud and solid career until one unavoidable but devastating tragedy rocked his world. In his desperate attempts to get off the streets, yet still save face, one little lie after another snowballed into a full-blown conspiracy that would cost him everything.

This is Officer Christopher Chung's story...

DECEPTION

Becoming a police officer was a goal of mine since I was a child. I used to idolize my father when he would come home from a long day of work in his uniform. I would always beg him to let me put on his uniform, although I knew it was clearly too big for me. I used to get so excited when I would wear his police hat and badge. My normal routine was walking around the neighborhood as if I was saving everyone. My parents had to literally force me to take that stuff off. I wore it during dinner and sometimes to bed. It was a great time growing up, but we lived in a different era. Back then, police officers were looked at as heroes. In today's society, it would be surprising to find many children who aspire to be police officers. Police officers have become the "bad guys" of society, according to mainstream and social media. The departments are scared to support their officers now because they do not want to stand up to angry mobs and news reporters who interrogate them about every single detail, when it comes to big stories. This lack of support is very disappointing and could end up ruining a good officer's career. This happened to me in 2012.

I usually patrolled the streets by myself, but would occasionally partner up with different officers when there were special tasks going on. These tasks included drug operations, gang takedowns and robbery stings. The tasks would come around every few months, because there were very big problems in South Philly. We were very busy and crime was taking over every single neighborhood. I always worked the graveyard shift because it gave me a steady schedule and allowed me to be home with my family during the day. It was also easy working this shift because the area wasn't too busy with traffic and other things at night. My fiancé, Kimberly, and I planned to get married in 2013. We were going to get married earlier, but we had just recently moved into an apartment building near 5th Street and Cheltenham Avenue and were still settling in.

The Philadelphia School District was diminished and the schools were terrible. We decided to send our two boys to private school, to ensure they were provided a proper education and a fair chance at life. Our ultimate goal was to get a home in the suburbs, but we really could not afford to do so at that time. It was funny because my sons were very different from me when I was their ages, which are ten and seven. I would be so fascinated with my father when he came home for work, but they were not the least bit interested in police work. They occasionally asked me about my equipment when they happened to glance at my belt, but that's about it. One of my sons always said he wanted to become a doctor when he grew up and the other wanted to own his own company. He never specified what type of company he wanted to own, he would just shoot off crazy ideas when Kim or I asked him about it. It was actually quite entertaining. Neither of the boys ever expressed any type of interest in law enforcement, which was somewhat disappointing. Kim was a high school teacher in Philadelphia and we always had conversations about the way kids are raised in today's society. She probably broke up more fights in her career than I did, because the kids were out of control. One day she came home and I wanted to speak to her about how kids were so spoiled in today's society.

"What happened to kids?"

"What do you mean? Are you referring to our kids?" She had a confused look on her face.

"No I'm referring to all kids, not just ours. They are so much different from when you and I were young. When I was a kid, all my friends wanted to either become pro athletes, police officers, firefighters or go to the military. Now it seems like kids don't want to do anything that involves physical activity. They just want to be all over social media."

"You're right, they don't. These are the times we live in, my dear. Even my students at school all want to be millionaires and business owners; they never mention jobs that involve labor anymore. They just imitate what they see on television."

She was absolutely right. That included my children as well. Although my children did not care too much about law enforcement, my family was very proud of me. I was happy with my career choice. I got along well with most of my coworkers and supervisors. I was fairly active, but my little niche was DUI traffic stops. I never really went looking for them, but for some reason I would always find them. My ultimate goal was to one-day get into the Traffic Unit, but I had a long way to go before I would have even gotten that opportunity. I did not really go out hunting for arrests like some of the other officers, because in this line of work danger always seemed to be right around the corner. That became true for me in April of 2012.

It was around 3:00 am when the radio call was dispatched for a robbery at 8th and Tasker Streets.

"All units be advised, we're getting a call for an armed robbery in progress, point of gun, in the area of 8th and Tasker. We have a female caller on the line, saying she was just robbed by a black male wearing a black hooded sweatshirt. The male displayed a black handgun, took her purse and was last seen running on 8th towards Reed."

I was on 10th and Wharton Streets checking up on one of our local businesses when the call came out. It was pouring rain when I got into my patrol car and began searching for the suspect. I drove right down to 8th Street because I knew if the suspect was still running this way he would come right towards me, because Wharton Street is only a few blocks down from Reed Street. I positioned my patrol car directly at the corner of the block, far back enough that the suspect would not see it if he was coming in this direction. I crept up to the corner house and peeked down 8th Street. As soon as I did this, I saw someone running up the street in a full sprint. He was wearing all black. Black hoodie, black jeans and black sneakers. I figured this had to be the suspect.

"Three Twenty One to dispatch, I believe I have the suspect running towards me on the corner of 8th and Wharton," I said in a low tone over the radio, so the suspect would not hear me.

"Three Twenty One, copy. All units be advised the suspect is possibly in the area of 8th and Wharton."

I was so nervous. I had been in several similar situations in my career but each one is just as scary as the last. Nothing really prepares you for these dangerous encounters. My heart was racing, the steady rain was beating down on top of my head and I was soaked. I took a deep breath and jumped out from behind the wall with my firearm pointed at the suspect.

"Police! Stop and let me see your hands."

Once he saw me jump out, the suspect immediately stopped. I could tell I startled him. He was tall and had a very solid build. I could not see his face because he had the hoodie pulled tight around his head. He stood there for a brief second holding something in his left hand. It was so dark outside and the rain seemed to be getting heavier, so it made it very difficult to see exactly what he was holding. I had a tight grip on my firearm, which was difficult because of the heavy rain. It was just him and I standing in the middle of 8th Street, like an Old Western showdown.

"Let me see your hands."

The suspect appeared to still be staring at me, but he was not following my directions. My nerves were getting the best of me because I could not tell what his next move was going to be and the weather made it very difficult to see clearly. The rain was just dripping down my face and in to my eyes. I did not see where his gun was and I did not want him to get an opportunity to get it out. All I wanted was for him to surrender without incident. In the distance, the sound of police sirens were getting closer to my location. The suspect heard this too because he immediately began looking around, as if he wanted to find an escape route.

"Listen buddy, I don't want to hurt you. Just show me your hands and don't do anything stupid."

It appeared the suspect was going to follow my directions at that point, so I took that opportunity to transmit over the radio to give them an update.

"Three Twenty One, I have the sus-" I was saying when I observed the suspect suddenly reach toward the right pocket of his hoodie.

"Don't do it."

He pulled a black object from the pocket. IT WAS A GUN.

Bang! Bang! Bang!

The sound of gunshots echoed in the air. My heart was beating so hard, I could actually feel it in my throat. I could not talk or move, I was in a complete state of shock. Other units pulled up and I was still holding my gun in the air, pointed towards the suspect. Everything seemed to be moving in slow motion and I did not know what to do after that. The rain was still pouring down and suddenly a hand grabbed my shoulder. I looked over and it was my sergeant. He saw that I was still shaking and he slowly took my gun from me. I looked down at my body to see if I was hit, but there was nothing. No blood, no pain and no graze wounds. I looked up at the suspect and he was laid out on the ground. I tried to walk over to the body, but my legs were not moving. I could only stare at his motionless body that was in the street and things slowly began to return to normal speed.

The sergeant transmitted over the radio "Three Bravo to dispatch, we have a police discharge down here. The suspect has been struck. Notify our detectives, and advise the Lieutenant that we will be taking the suspect directly to Jefferson Hospital."

"Three Bravo received."

The sergeant instructed other officers on the scene to pick up the suspect and drive him to the hospital.

"We have no time to wait for the medics to come. Get him to the hospital now."

"Three Bravo to dispatch, notify Jefferson Hospital that two of our units are in route to their location with the suspect. Make sure they have their staff ready for him."

"Three Bravo received. They have been advised."

I watched as the suspect was placed into the back of the patrol car. He did not appear to be moving and I was still in shock. It happened so fast and I was not ready for the emotions that followed a shooting.

"Sarge, there is a gun and the victim's purse that were next to the suspect's body," one of the officers said to the sergeant.

"Ok. Leave it there. The detectives should be here any minute to start processing this scene."

I stood in the same spot for a while. My heartbeat began to normalize and my brain began to process everything that just took place. It was unreal. I could not believe I just shot someone. In the back of my head, I knew that there was a possibility of this happening once I put on the uniform every day, but I never expected it to actually happen to me. I do not think anyone expects it. My father spent thirty years on the job and never had to shoot anyone. I wanted a similar career, because I was a god fearing man and did not truly believe in taking a life. We were trained to shoot at center mass because aiming at limbs increased the chance of missing and hitting innocent civilians. Nevertheless, aiming at center mass also meant the chance your target would survive was very slim. I stood there watching the pool of the suspect's blood being washed up by the heavy rain and flowing right into the sewer drain. I know I did my job by eliminating a possible threat, but I did not feel good about it at all. I told him repeatedly to show me his hand. I wish he just listened to me.

"Are you ok?" the sergeant asked me.

"No not really."

"Well listen, I have to take you to be interviewed by the Homicide Detectives because they investigate all police involved shootings, alongside Internal Affairs."

"Does this mean the suspect died?"

"No, this is just the department's protocol."

"Ok."

The sergeant instructed another officer to take my patrol car back to the district and I rode with him down to Police Headquarters, where the Homicide Division is located. As we pulled off, I watched as detectives arrived on location, taking pictures of the scene and collecting the evidence. My uniform was soaking wet from the rain and I was shivering. My hands were still shaking and my nerves were killing me.

I sat down at Police Headquarters for about two hours, before I was interviewed. I was informed the investigating detectives were at the scene and going to the hospital and I had to wait for them to come back. I was so nervous. I could not help but wonder if the suspect was all right. I do not know if most cops thought like this but I actually shared compassion for all people, no matter who they were or what they did. Everybody does things for a reason and you should not have to die for making a mistake. That is why I kept telling him to show me his hands. The more I waited, the more nervous I became. My one concern was not bothering me because I was completely sure he had a gun. That is one of the main issues in police shootings, whether the suspect truly had a weapon or not and my suspect did. I know that for sure. I saw him pull it from his pocket and the officer at the scene told the sergeant it was on the ground, so I was not worried about that part of it. I just had to patiently wait for the investigators to return.

After my two hour wait, the investigators came walking in, and two of them pulled me into an interview room. The room was outdated and had a very eerie feeling to it. There were stains on the ceiling and cracks on the wall. The chair I had to sit in was wobbly and barely standing up. I was still soaked, even after my long wait. I sat down and placed my hands on the table. Once I looked down at the table, I immediately removed my hands. The table was disgusting. It had a slot where you would handcuff a prisoner to and it was all rusted out. There was dry blood around it and I wanted my hands nowhere near that disgusting area. I placed my hands on my lap and had my head down the entire time, because I did not have a good feeling about anything that occurred that night.

One of the investigators started out by saying, "How are you doing, officer? I am Sergeant Mason with the Homicide Division. This is Lieutenant Rodgers from Internal Affairs. We just want to speak to you about the shooting that occurred today."

"Is the suspect ok? That's my only concern, sir."

"Well, we will get to that. But first just tell us what happened," Lieutenant Rodgers said.

"Ok. I was patrolling tonight, technically this morning, and around three o clock an armed robbery call came out. The robbery was at 8th and Tasker and I was at 10th and Wharton. The information provided was that the suspect was last seen running on 8th Street in a black hoodie. I went to 8th Street and sure enough, the suspect was running right towards me. I hopped out on him and begged him to show me his hands. I promise you I asked him probably three times to show me his hand. All I wanted him to do was show me his hands and I wouldn't have shot him." I began getting very emotional and I guess the sergeant noticed that.

"Officer Chung, it's going to be ok. Just tell us exactly what happened."

"Alright. I had him at gunpoint, asking him to show me his hands. Initially he did. He showed me his hands. However, as the other units could be heard coming towards us, it seemed like he panicked and wanted to run. I was still focused on him and his hands were up. He had something in his left hand but I could not really see what it was because of the way he was holding it, but I knew that was not a gun or weapon. Well I didn't really know, I just figured it wasn't because of the way it was being held. When I reached down towards my radio microphone to let the dispatcher know I had him stopped, that's when he reached for the gun with his right hand. I saw him pull it out from his pocket and it was definitely a gun. I know it was raining hard but I am a hundred percent sure about it and that is when I fired my weapon. After that, I froze and everybody else arrived. I know our policy says we are supposed to immediately handcuff the suspect even if they are shot, but I was scared and couldn't move. I am not afraid to admit that. It was the first time I ever had to do something like that and I was scared." My eyes began to tear up just from the mere fact I had to explain the incident in detail.

"Ok officer, everything sounds legitimate, so you really don't have anything to worry about when it comes to the department. The evidence at the scene confirmed everything you said to us. We found the gun and we also found the victim's purse that the suspect had taken. You were justified in taking the shot."

"So what now? Is he going to be taken to jail? How bad are his injuries?"

I watched as the sergeant put his head down before responding to me. I looked over at the Lieutenant and he avoided all eye contact with me. At that moment, I knew the news was not going to be good.

"Officer Chung, the suspect was pronounced dead at the hospital."

When he said that, I slammed my head on the table. "No, no, no. That can't be true. They took him to the hospital. They didn't hesitate or wait; they took him right to the hospital, so how could he have died?"

"He had three gunshot wounds to the chest. There was nothing the doctors could do for him at that point."

I was beside myself and they could tell how emotional I was.

"There's something else you should know" Lieutenant Rodgers said.

"What?"

"The suspect was only fourteen years old."

I literally fell out of the chair. Tears began falling from my eyes and I slammed my fists on the ground.

"Fourteen? He was only fourteen? I killed a fourteen year old?"

I was completely done. Nothing could calm me down at that moment because I just took the life of a child.

"Where the hell did a fourteen year old get a gun from?"

Sergeant Mason placed an evidence bag on the table. I looked at the bag and it contained the gun.

"It's a BB gun," he informed me.

I looked at him and my mouth dropped to the floor. Are you freaking serious? The gun looked so real. It literally looked like a real gun and not a toy. I felt like I was having a heart attack. I was on the ground holding my chest, as they tried to calm me down.

"Officer Chung 'listen, you didn't know. You couldn't tell the kid was fourteen and you wouldn't have known he only had a BB gun. We interviewed the victim first and she thought he was in his mid-twenties and was also surprised to hear that he only had a BB gun. She thought it was a real gun too, when he pointed it at her. The orange tip of the BB gun was spray painted black, which gave it a very real appearance."

I heard him loud and clear but the only words that stood out to me were "fourteen" and "BB gun." The pain in my chest worsened and the sergeant ended up calling the paramedics to take me to the hospital. The paramedics responded to the building and transported me to Penn Hospital, because they did not want me to be at Jefferson where the suspect's family would be. I ended up having to stay overnight at the hospital because of the pain. The doctor diagnosed me with stress related chest pain, which has similar symptoms to a heart attack. The department contacted my wife and she came to the hospital to be by my side.

"Your sergeant called and told me what happened Chris. How are you?"

"Did he tell you everything?"

"Yes."

"Did he tell you I shot a robbery suspect, who was only a kid?"

"Yes he did. Everything's going to be just fine, he said you didn't do anything wrong."

"I didn't do anything wrong? I killed a kid Kim, that's far from right."

"I know Chris, but it wasn't a cold-blooded murder. You were doing your job."

"My job is to protect and serve, not to play god and take lives."

She tried to comfort me but no matter what anyone said regarding me making a right or wrong decision, the fact is a kid lost his life. The simple fact that the suspect was a kid haunted me for months. After I was released from the hospital, I had to take a couple weeks off work to get myself together mentally and emotionally. Many people tried to reach out to me, asking how I was feeling but it was hard for me to speak about the situation. I figured in order to get over the situation, I had to just put it behind me and move forward. It was bad enough the shooting was all over the news; I did not want to keep talking about it and explaining myself. The media's headlines all said the same thing, "Philadelphia police officer shoots teenager who had a BB gun." It was truly heartbreaking seeing the reactions people had on every news station, the biased opinions and seeing the suspect's family all over television. I was a father, so every time I looked at my sons I thought about him. No type of training the department offered prepared me for this moment.

The shooting had a terrible impact on my life. I could not sleep because I would always dream about that night repeatedly. I refused to turn on the television because I would tear up every time I saw his face on the news. There were even reports that came out that exposed the suspect's violent criminal history. This was not the first time he robbed someone or possessed a gun. This information didn't make me feel any better, because he was still just a kid. We all made foolish mistakes as kids.

The slightest banging noise would startle me, reminding me of those three gunshots. I was a mess over this whole misfortune. Kim noticed a significant change in my attitude and behavior. In an attempt to help out, she scheduled an appointment with a psychiatrist. This would have been ideal, if I was ready to open up about the situation but I wasn't at the time. I would have given anything in the world to rewind back to that night and I would not have even drew my firearm. I would have just tackled the suspect instead. Depression and guilt consumed me. I was constantly wishing I would have known the gun was not real. Wishing I would have known he was just a child. I would have never pulled that trigger. It was bad enough dealing with the shooting mentally, but after weeks of coverage the media released my name all over the news. When this happened, everything went from bad to worse. Random people and reporters were calling our phones and showing up outside our apartment. My family's privacy was being invaded and there was nothing we could do about it. The police department did not take any of this into consideration either. I contacted them several times and I always got the run around. They were not publicly defending me. They just allowed the media to tarnish my name, even though I did nothing wrong. It even affected Kim at work. She came home in tears one day after being reassigned and having her classroom given to another teacher. The look on her face when she walked in said it all.

"What's wrong Kim?"

"I got reassigned to an administrative position in the school's office."

"Why would they reassign you? Did you do something wrong?"

She did not immediately respond and hung her head down. I knew the problem could not have been with her. It had to be all the media attention that was the cause of her reassignment.

"Is it because of the shooting?"

"Yes."

"But what does it have to do with you and the school?"

"Apparently one of the parents saw your name and face all over the news. They found out that I was your wife, after watching the news and decided they didn't want me around their child. They ended up calling the principal today and I got my classroom taken away from me."

"Are they even allowed to do that?"

"You know they can do whatever they want, especially if they get complaints from parents."

"Well I'm sorry. I just wish none of this happened."

"Don't you dare apologize for anything Chris. This is in no way your fault. You did your job and you did it right. We will find a way to get through all of this."

There had to be something I could do. I called my sergeant and the union representative, but nobody wanted to help me. The media never gave all the details surrounding the shooting, so once they released my information it seemed like I was guilty of a crime. They tried to use so many angles to paint a negative picture of me. The most frequent angle they used was racism. They questioned whether race played any part in the shooting, which it didn't at all. I could not believe they were allowed to do this. Now most of the staff and parents at Kim's job probably thought she was married to a racist murderer. I requested the city do some type of press conference to tell everyone I did not do anything wrong, but the investigation was still open so they refused to do any type of press conference. It did not matter to them that my life had fallen apart. I was helpless for the next six months. During that time, I also received a new assignment at work because they still had possession of my firearm for the investigation. So once I was ready to return to work, it would be at the 3rd District.

When I returned to work, things were very different. I was assigned to the Real Time Crime Division, which was in charge of monitoring surveillance footage throughout the city. That division would assist patrol units when they were looking for suspects and vehicles that had fled from a crime scene. I did not even know this division existed prior to my assignment. It was a complete upgrade from working the dangerous streets every day. My duty firearm was confiscated, so I had no other choice than to work inside. This was the usual protocol for officers that were involved in shootings, until the internal affairs investigation was complete and officers were cleared of any wrongdoing. This was the case in my shooting. I spent months in the Real Time Crime Division before I was finally cleared. During that time, the media continued covering the story and I was constantly questioned by coworkers about the entire incident. I tried my best to avoid the repetitive questions but when I could not avoid them, my favorite reply was "I can't talk about an ongoing investigation." That usually did the trick. I actually got acquainted with a Corporal in the division. That was his permanent assignment and he seemed to love working there. I asked him about the possibility of keeping the assignment since I was cleared and his response was not really what I was looking for.

“So is everyone that comes down here under investigation?”

"No. Most of us volunteered for this division because it was recently created and seemed to be an intuitive advancement in investigating crimes. You have been the fourth person we had temporarily because of an investigation."

"Well I like it here. What are the chances they allow me to stay here?"

"Well to be honest, the chances are very slim."

"Why is that?"

"Real Crime is a great division to work in and there is an extremely long waiting list. So unless you know someone that can get you at the top of that list, you're going to have to apply and hope you get a chance, like everybody else."

"Wow. That's never going to happen."

"The only other way is if you get shot. You'll be able to come right in here," the Corporal said in a joking manner.

"What do you mean?"

"You never heard that if you get shot on the job, you get to handpick where you want to go and they let you go there immediately?"

"No I never heard that before."

"Well that's the reward you get for something bad happening to you. That's a one way ticket to any division or unit in the department."

That was a very interesting conversation. I guess since the investigation was complete, I would be headed back to the 3rd District. I really didn't think that would be a good idea because the suspect's family lived in South Philly and I wouldn't be able to see any of them without being reminded of the tragedy. Even after the investigation, the department never released anything to the media to clear my name. The only information they provided was that I was cleared to return to full duty. That was not good enough. I needed them to release the details of the robbery and the fact I gave the suspect more than enough chances to surrender. That never happened. I dreaded the day of my return back to the district. As the months went by, I became very comfortable in the division and loved every minute of it. Work actually became my escape from the depression because the media continued harassing us at our home.

I finally received the notice from the department that I was to return to the 3rd District. It was dreadful from the moment I stepped in the door. I received mixed greetings from everyone. Some were glad to see me back on duty and others side-eyed me and didn't say a word. Most of the side-eyes came from black officers. I was not really surprised after the media attempted to make the shooting a racial issue. I am sure some of the black officers were wondering in their minds if any of the allegations were true. This caused a lot of weird tension between them and myself. There were occasions when I would be on domestic disturbance calls, where I had two people fighting, and my back up never showed up. This made me realize that my general safety was even more at risk when I got to work and I wanted out of the 3rd District. Things were getting worse before they got any better. On top of dealing with these false allegations against me, I had to deal with the fact I was still having nightmares of the shooting. I thought I would be over it by now, but it never left my memory. Although I was never in a situation that was as dangerous as the shooting, hesitation seemed to play a major part in my encounters with the public. I was hesitant to get involved in escalating situations and other officers noticed this. I would usually stand off to the side and let other officers take charge. This eventually led to me not purposely driving directly to certain radio calls, so

I would not be the first officer on scene. The next thing I knew, I was being called into the sergeant's office to discuss this issue.

"What's going on Chris?"

"Nothing much sir, just getting used to the streets again."

"That's good. How are you mentally, with everything that took place?"

"I'm ok. I don't get that much sleep because I have nightmares all the time."

"Did you talk to your doctor about that?"

"Yea, I did. I actually went to go see a psychiatrist about the entire situation, but that didn't help at all."

"That's a shame. Well I called you in here because some concerns have been brought to my attention."

"What concerns would that be?"

"Some of your fellow officers have been complaining that you aren't doing your job. I understand you have experienced a traumatic event, but you still have a duty to protect the community members and your coworkers."

"I'm doing my job sir. I just don't want to end up in a bad situation again."

"I understand that. Do you want to be here?"

"What are you asking? Do I want to be in the district?"

'Do you want to continue doing police work?"

"To be completely honest with you, I don't really want to work the streets anymore. I rather be in a division like Real Time Crime."

"Well, I suggest you apply to get in that division, but in the mean time you still have to do your job when you come to work. I can help you out by asking the Lieutenant to assign you to an inside position, but it's not going to be a guarantee that he will allow it."

"That would help a lot and I would appreciate that."

"Ok. I'll see what I can do."

After that conversation with the sergeant, I discovered the Lieutenant denied me. I believed I was denied because the staff inside did not want to work with me. That showed me that I had to do something to get out of the district. If it were that obvious that I was not stepping up and doing my job, it would not be long before the supervisor would take disciplinary action against me. There was no other alternatives left for me to try. I was exhausted and completely stressed out.

I thought long and hard of ways to get out of the district and off the streets. The department denied me the opportunity to continue working with the Real Time Crime Division and the district denied me the opportunity of working inside the control center or prisoner intake area. As an outcast in the district, I had no options left. The only thing that guaranteed me a spot to go anywhere would be me being shot. It had to happen. The decision was made and I planned on going through with it. I was at work on a cool fall night and pulled over in the area of 6th and Federal Streets. I exited my patrol vehicle and drew my firearm from the holster. I held my firearm up against my head and thought about ending it all. I could not do it, so I pointed it directly at my vest. I took a deep breath and closed my eyes. My finger slowly squeezed on the trigger and suddenly, BANG. The loud shot caused my ears to ring, as I fell back onto the cold concrete ground. My firearm had fallen out my hand and a sharp pain passed through my abdominal area. The back of my head hit the ground as I fell. The cold concrete sent chills through the back of my head, as I struggled to get to the radio microphone.

"Three Twenty One to dispatch. Officer down. I've been shot."

"What's your location Three Twenty One?"

"I'm at 6th and Federal."

"All units be advised we have an officer down at 6th and Federal. EMS has been advised. I repeat all units be advised we have an officer down at 6th and Federal."

The next thing I heard was an officer transmitting over the radio. "Three Twenty Four to dispatch I'm right around the corner."

An officer immediately arrived on location in seconds. She pulled up to me and exited her patrol car with her firearm drawn, scanning the area for suspects.

"Where is the suspect?"

I did not expect her to get to me that fast, so I had to think of something quick.

"They ran off. It was two of them."

"Which way did they run? What did they look like?"

"Up to 7th Street. It was two black guys. They had short dreadlocks or braids. I'm not too sure because it happened so fast."

She continued scanning the area, focusing towards 7th Street.

"Three Twenty Four to Dispatch, the suspects are two black males with braids or dreadlocks. They ran up to 7th Street."

"All units be advised, an update on the officer down in the area of 6th and Federal. We are searching for two suspects. They are described as two black males with braids or dreadlocks. They were last seen running on Federal towards 7th Street."

A few minutes went by and the sergeant arrived on scene at the same time as the paramedics. They all approached me and began checking me out.

"It hurts so bad."

"It looks like the shot hit your vest only. You're a very lucky man," one of the paramedics said as he examined my abdomen.

"So why does it hurt so bad if I'm so lucky?"

"It looks like you have some bruising from the impact of the shot. I wouldn't be surprised if you have a broken rib or two."

I was placed into the ambulance and transported to Penn Hospital. Once I got to the hospital, a barrage of police personnel poured in after me. Everyone from the police commissioner to other 3rd District officers came in to check on me. This is exactly what I needed. I would definitely be able to be transferred now. Inside I was so happy because all the negative attention I was receiving from my initial shooting had now turned into sympathy. I had to get x-rays to ensure I did not have any broken ribs. Everything came back negative and it seemed like the pain and bruising was the worst I had to deal with. Once the x-rays were complete, I was taken back to a room where my whole command staff was waiting to question me.

As soon as I got into the room, there was an investigator from the Pennsylvania State Police and detectives gathering my uniform and ballistic vest. The investigator performed a gunshot residue test on my hands. I did not think anything of it because I was mentally focused on which unit I wanted to transfer to. This was my chance to get into the Traffic Unit, but I had really gotten used to the Real Time Crime Division. My mind was totally on those two units and suddenly Kim showed up to the hospital with the kids.

"Oh my god, what happened Chris? Are you ok?"

"I just got shot by some thugs tonight baby, but I'm all right."

"Where was this? What were you doing?"

"It was down 6th and Federal. I was just on Patrol and they came out of nowhere and shot me."

"I heard that the police are looking for two guys. It's all over the news."

"It is? What are they saying?"

"The news said Philly PD and the State Police are doing a full out manhunt for the guys that shot you."

"Really?"

"Yes. It's crazy. There are helicopters out and everything. I'm just so glad you are ok. I don't know what I would do if I lost you."

"Kim, trust me everything is going to be ok?"

"I hope so," she said as tears were still running down her cheek.

I felt bad for lying to her, but I could not tell her the truth at that time. I was able to spend a significant amount of time with Kim and the kids before I had to be interviewed by the investigators. We did not really explain to the kids everything that was going on. I thought it would be too upsetting trying to explain the fact their dad could have died tonight. For that brief moment, I felt like someone important. My family and I got to meet the mayor, police commissioner and the deputy commissioners. It was exciting being around the city's top dogs. Finally, my time was up and it was time to speak with the investigators.

There were three investigators that came into the room. They allowed Kim and the kids to stay by my side while they questioned me. Sergeant Mason from the Homicide Division walked in the room.

"Hello Officer Chung, I'm sure you remember me from our interview months ago."

"Yes I do. How are you doing Sergeant Mason?"

"I am good. The question is how are you doing?"

"I'm just happy to be alive sir."

“That’s definitely a blessing. I know it’s very soon, but I just need to ask you a few more details about the suspects because we have a major manhunt taking place and we really want to catch these guys.”

“Ok sure.” I was nervous because I was not expecting to be questioned almost immediately after the incident occurred.

‘Let’s start with the suspects’ description. I need as much detail about them as possible that you can remember.”

“Well I didn’t really get a good look at them. I know they were black guys and had short dreadlocks or braids. I could not really tell because it was dark out. They were definitely wearing hoodies. But that’s all I remember.”

“How about any facial hair or tattoos?”

“Umm yeah they had facial hair. They both had beards and one of them had a tattoo on his face but I couldn’t see what it was.”

“What complexion were they? Light or dark?”

“I would say they had medium complexions.”

“Are you sure they were black? Could they have been Hispanic?”

“No they were definitely black guys.”

“How about their voices. Did either of them say anything to you?”

“No, they just ran up on me.”

“If you don’t mind, can you tell me the events that led up to the shooting?”

“I was patrolling in the area of 6th and Federal and I pulled over to run a tag on a vehicle I was behind at the time. As soon as I ran the tag, they ran up on me and one of them stuck a gun through the window. I opened my door and we began struggling. I drew my firearm and the next thing I know, a shot was fired. I felt the pain to my abdominal area and I fell to the ground. That's when they both ran off."

"So let me get this straight you opened the door and began wrestling with both suspects?"

"Yes, that's correct."

"And only one shot was fired?"

"Yes, the shot that hit me."

"So you were ambushed by two suspects and they just ran away after you hit the ground? They didn't take anything or try to shoot you again?"

"You know what Sarge, my stomach is starting to hurt. I need to get some rest. Can we continue this another time?"

"Yes, I think we have enough information to continue the search for the suspects. We will definitely be in touch."

I was so relieved when Sergeant Mason concluded the interview because I think he saw right through my deception. I was making it all up, as he asked each question and was not doing such a good job at it. I had to develop a solid story that was going to be believable. I planned to do that once I got home from the hospital, which ended up being the same night. The doctor came in about an hour after Sergeant Mason left and informed me I would not have to stay overnight because all I had was bruising. Upon my discharge from the hospital, the Police Commissioner told me to contact him when I was cleared to return to work. This had to be the opportunity I wanted. My plan seemed like it worked. I was going to request to return to the Real Time Crime Division or the Traffic Unit. The media was stationed outside the hospital and we waited a few hours to leave because we did not feel like being harassed by reporters. Once we got home, I thought long and hard about telling Kim the truth. She was so concerned about me and I did not want her to truly be worried. She had taken some time off work just to be with me while I recovered. The more I thought about it, the more I was not too sure if she would understand the method behind the decision I made.

The next morning, I received a phone call from Sergeant Mason. He had a few follow up questions for me, but I brushed him off with claims of pain. I figured the more time I waited, the less they would keep looking for these suspects that didn't really exist. Things did not really work out as planned because he ended up showing up to my home unexpectedly the next day. I was laying on the couch in the living room when Kim told me he was here. I walked into the dining room to sit with Sergeant Mason and the two other investigators that were with him at the hospital.

"Hello Officer Chung. I know when we spoke on the phone yesterday you said you weren't feeling to well, but there's something we need done."

He placed numerous photographs on the table and spread them out. They appeared to be mug shots of black males.

"What are these?"

"These are photographs of local gang members in the South Philly area. A few of them were detained in relation to the manhunt for your suspects and I wanted to know if anyone looked familiar."

"No, I don't think it was any of these guys."

"But you didn't even look at the photographs."

"Well, I told you at the hospital that I didn't get a good look at their faces."

"But you also said they had dreadlocks, beards and one had a face tattoo, so I'm sure at least looking at the photographs may help refresh your memory."

I skimmed through the photographs at the dozens of men who actually fit the description of my fictitious suspects. I began realizing that I may have been in over my head because they were obviously serious about the manhunt.

"I don't see the suspects."

"Are you sure? We have half of the department, and the State Police out looking for your shooter and we're trying to get in touch with the FBI for some assistance."

"The FBI? That is not necessary. I am ok. I was only shot in my vest, it's not like I was killed."

"Oh it's definitely necessary. No one is going to shoot an officer and get away with it."

I was very uncomfortable, but could not think of a way to get Sergeant Mason to stop badgering me about finding the suspects.

"So are we done here?"

"No, I just have one more question for you. You said the suspects took one shot at you, but you never mentioned you taking a shot back at them. Why were you missing a round from your firearm?"

"Umm, I must have shot a round off during the struggle."

"Must have? You aren't sure?"

"No, like I said things happened so fast that night."

Sergeant Mason looked at me with a very doubtful expression on his face. I was sure he knew something was not right with my story.

"Is there anything you need to tell me Officer Chung?"

This was my chance to come clean and tell the truth about everything.

"No. There's nothing I need to tell you."

Sergeant Mason and the other investigators collected their photographs and left. This was not good. They had suspects detained and were considering bringing in the FBI. My plan did not seem to working very well and I was concerned. Kim had a concerned look on her face too, as she overheard the questioning from Sergeant Mason. Kim picked up her iPad and scrolled to something. Seconds later, she placed the iPad on the table in front of me and walked out of the dining room. I looked down and observed the 6abc app she opened. It was displaying the story about the manhunt. I wondered if she figured out that I wasn't being completely honest about the ambush. After that evening, Kim never asked me about the ambush and things seemed to be going well. I did not hear from Sergeant Mason for a while. Although weeks were passing, the media still reported on the incident. I honestly thought I was in the clear and I was scheduled to return to work in two months. My plan was to call the Police Commissioner and ask him if it was possible to be transferred upon my return. Sergeant Mason interrupted that plan.

I will never forget when he stopped by on a Monday morning. Kim was at work and the kids were at school. I was home relaxing when I heard a very loud knock at the door. I answered the door and once again, it was Sergeant Mason and the investigators.

"Officer Chung, we need to speak with you."

"Ok, come on in."

We walked right back to the dining room and sat down. This time Sergeant Mason placed an evidence box on the table and began taking folders out. Each folder was pretty thick and contained a lot of paperwork. I sat at the table as my nerves got the best of me. My right foot kept tapping the floor, my teeth were grinding and my palms were sweaty. I had no idea what was in the folders, but it could not have been good.

"We have something we need to discuss."

"What would that be?" My voice was cracking.

"There are some inconsistencies in your story compared to our evidence."

"What do you mean by inconsistencies?"

"I mean there were no witnesses, no camera footage at the scene, no full suspect description, no other shell casing from any firearm besides yours and other inconsistencies."

I stood up and grabbed a bottle of water from the refrigerator. As I drank, I attempted to think of a way I could help support my allegations. My head was about to explode, because I was thinking about all the lies I already told and I could not remember exactly what I said. I was also thinking about my initial shooting, which started this whole thing. I was a complete mess.

"So are you accusing me of lying, Sergeant?"

"The last time we spoke, I gave you the opportunity to tell me the truth and you didn't."

"I told you. I didn't remember anything."

"I know exactly what you told me, so now let me tell you something. We looked at footage from convenience stores and other businesses in the area. At the time you claimed you were ambushed, the footage shows no one running up or down Federal Street. That meant either they ran down 6th Street and you were confused or there were no suspects. That prompted us to test your hands for gunpowder residue, which was done at the hospital. It took a while for the results to come back, but for some reason they matched the same residue found on your uniform shirt and the results were an exact match to the department's ammunition."

I could not take it anymore. I was caught red handed.

"Please give me a chance to explain why I did it."

Sergeant Mason looked very frustrated and yelled, "I gave you that chance already. Do you know how many men and women have spent the past three weeks looking for suspects that don't exist? Do you know how many resources we used during this investigation? I don't want to hear your pathetic explanation. You are a sorry excuse of an officer and don't deserve to wear a badge."

"I'm sorry but I had to do it. I had to get off the streets."

"Listen we need you to come with us. I will give you the benefit of the doubt and not drag you out in cuffs in front of your neighbors, but you have to come with us."

"Where are we going?"

"We're going to go to Internal Affairs, so you can make an official statement."

"Will I get a chance to call my wife?"

"If you cooperate with us, we will cooperate with you."

At that moment, I knew it was all over. The only thing left to do was to face the consequences of my actions. I knew Kim and the kids would be devastated when they found out what really happened. My family was going to be very disappointed and embarrassed, especially my father. I ended up locking up the house and going with Sergeant Mason to Internal Affairs. Once I got there, I was very cooperative and told them the truth about everything.

Officer Christopher Chung was arrested and charged with making a false report to law enforcement. He was terminated from the Philadelphia Police Department and sentenced to two years in prison. Chung has since been released from prison and is still working towards paying off the costs of the investigation and manhunt that followed his false report.

CHAPTER EIGHT

Detective Erica Giordano was a three-year veteran of the Philadelphia Police Department. She was born and raised in South Philadelphia. Erica attended South Philadelphia High School and afterwards the Community College of Philadelphia, where she obtained an Associate's Degree in Justice. After obtaining her Associates degree, Erica continued her studies at Temple University, where she obtained her Master's Degree in Criminal Justice. Upon graduation, she followed the family tradition of law enforcers and applied to become a Philadelphia police officer. She completed the police academy in 2011 and served as a patrol officer in the 2nd District which covers the Northeast section of Philadelphia. After serving only two years in Patrol, Erica was promoted to the rank of detective for Northeast Detective Division. She was on the fast-track to a stellar career, but that all came crashing down the day her love for the law clashed with the love of her life. It's a fine line between helping a loved one out of a jam... and active conspiracy with the mob. Especially when the FBI is watching.

This is Detective Erica Giordano's story...

Growing up, I was destined to become a police officer. I had so many uncles, cousins and friends that were in all different ranks of the Philadelphia Police Department, as well as ones that were retired. I could have gotten the job straight out of high school, but I always wanted to obtain a degree first. Once I got the job, things went according to plan. My uncle was a chief inspector and he pulled some strings to make sure I wasn't stuck in one of the more dangerous districts. It was very good having perks and it seemed like I needed them because I was a small girl that everyone side eyed because of my stature. I was only five foot five and weighed a hundred and twenty five pounds. Although I was in shape, I already knew how the majority of men felt about women officers. I used to hear all the jokes and chauvinistic viewpoints during family gatherings, so I could only imagine what my male co-workers thought about me. Once I got to the 2nd District, I was assigned to work with Officer Jessica Scorelli. This was good because she was a family friend and I knew her for years. Her dad was a retired captain and she actually dated one of my brothers when they were in high school. She normally worked inside the control center, but made an exception to go back on the streets to train me.

I learned so much working with Jess. She told me about the people I needed to keep an eye on, whether on the streets or in the district. She had five years of experience when I got to the district, so she knew all the ups and downs of the department. We worked hard and played hard too. We often went to gatherings at the FOP Lodge 5 and we frequented bars all around the city. I was somewhat of a little social butterfly and she was a party animal. After about six months on the street, Jess and I talked about working inside the district. Working inside was much safer and we didn't have to wear that duty belt that killed my back. There was a little jealousy in the district from my co-workers because I was allowed to work inside the control center so early in my career. I couldn't help that the captain was friends with my uncle and I got the special treatment they wished they had. Once I began working inside, coming to work was a breeze. We didn't have to deal with the troubles on the street and we also got to work with each other every day. Jess planned to take the detective promotional exam and she talked me into taking it with her. We had a whole year to study, which was easy because we did a lot of that on duty. We were able to study the department's directives and all the assigned books during our downtime. We ending up taking the detective exam in the fall of 2012 and I immediately called my uncle and let him know we took it. We were promoted the next year and Jessica and I were both assigned to the Northeast Detectives, which meant we would work out the same building and we would stay together. Not many of our co-workers were happy for us but I could care less.

They would always make smart remarks like, "You have to put more time in on the street," "This job is learned on the streets and not in books," "Fresh out the academy and straight into detectives," "Silver spooners" and other jealous things. This really had no effect on me because I looked at it as pure envy.

Our first day on as detectives was the best experience ever. It felt so good coming to work dressed professionally and not in that ugly uniform. We were in training for the first month. We learned the duties of an investigator, the things to look for at a crime scene and the way to conduct interviews. Although it didn't initially seem that way, detective work was completely different than patrol work. I felt right at home because obviously I was more brain than brawn. I believed I could be very productive as an investigator and I was good with paperwork too. Jess was having a great time too. She was doing very well and all we talked about was when the day would come when we would get to investigate crimes side by side.

My first investigation was a commercial burglary of the Lowes on Academy Road. I was working under Detective William Graham, who was a sixteen-year veteran of the department. He showed me the ropes and prepared me to be on my own. He told me there had been a rash of commercial burglaries going on around the city and in the surrounded suburbs.

In each case, a hardware store was burglarized and the suspects stole tools and electronics. We were working to see if there was a connection between our burglary and the others. If there were a connection, we would have to contact the Major Crimes Unit and work alongside of them. In our job, it was reported that possibly five subjects broke into the Lowes overnight, when employees were stocking in the rear of the store. William gave me the task of skimming through the surveillance footage from Lowes. My job was to find something that would lead us to the suspects.

As I looked through the footage, nothing stood out. You couldn't see the suspects' faces because they had on masks and appeared to know exactly where the cameras were located. The intruders moved in a quick stealth mode, you could tell they were professionals. Even when viewing the footage from the exterior of the store, they didn't park their getaway vehicle in the sight of the camera until they were ready to load it up. Nothing stood out about the vehicle either. It was a black work van, possibly a Ford E-250 or similar vehicle. I spent the entire shift looking through footage and came up with nothing. I was somewhat disappointed and thought William was going to be to, but he wasn't. He just told me we would continue looking until we found something. After work, Jess and I went out to have a few drinks. This became a regular routine for us and was our little escape from work. While we were out, we saw a few people from the district. They spent the whole night hitting on us and buying us drinks. We had a good time, but it was somewhat awkward because all they talked about was work stuff. I always had the mentality that once I left work, I didn't want to talk or even think about it. I was just out to have a good time. We wrapped the night up early because we had work the next day.

The next morning started with me assisting William with a search warrant service. We were serving a search warrant at a suspect's home, who was involved in a theft from a neighborhood school. The suspect lived on Large Street, off Unruh Avenue. It was a normal two-story row home, at the end of the block. William called for a uniformed officer to assist us and it happened to be someone I graduated the academy with. Officer Matthew Yerges and I were not only in the same academy class, but also in the same platoon. He was a very nice guy in the academy and it was good seeing him. I loved seeing classmates while I worked because they always wanted to talk about me being promoted so early. William knocked on the front door and the suspect's mother answered the door.

"Yes, can I help you?" the woman asked.

William introduced us. "Hello ma'am, we're Detectives Graham and Giordano. We have a search warrant to enter your residence to search for evidence from a crime. We're investigating a possible theft that was committed by your son."

"I knew it. I knew that boy was up to no good," she said. "Come right on in. His room is in the basement."

We gave her a copy of the report and we began searching. We were looking for an Apple MacBook and iPad, which had been stolen from one of the teachers. As we looked through the basement, we found several electronics that appeared to be stolen. There were iPods, multiple tablets, GPS devices and digital cameras. I collected the items and William began questioning me.

"What are you doing with those?"

"I'm taking them because they're stolen."

"How do you know they're stolen?"

"Because I know they aren't his."

William stopped what he was doing and asked me, "Do you have any proof they aren't his?"

"No I don't..." I began replying until I was suddenly cut off.

"Well, put the stuff back. Yes, they're probably stolen, but until we can confirm that we can't take them," William said. "What you can do is document the suspected stolen items and their serial numbers, so we can add them to the report."

I did just that and it took forever. While I was documenting all the items, I suddenly heard "Found them."

I looked up and William appeared to be jumping for joy. He had the stolen items we were looking for in his hands. We went upstairs and informed the suspect's mother what we found. She wasn't the least bit surprised either. William began asking her about the whereabouts of her son, but she claimed she didn't know where he was. We left the home and Matt and I continued talking. He attempted to ask me out on a date, but I wasn't interested. It was something about growing up with a bunch of cops that made me never want to date one. Plus, I was attracted to men with facial hair and most cops weren't allowed to have any. I did take his number because I didn't want to seem rude, but I knew I wasn't going to use it. William and I went back to the district with our evidence and William had me log it in, while he started typing the criminal complaint for the suspect. After logging in the evidence, I went back to viewing the footage again from the Lowes burglary. That took up the rest of my shift and once again, I was left with nothing. When the shift was over, I was all alone because Jess was stuck on another investigation. I had no other choice but to just go home and keep myself occupied. This became a routine for me. I would either go to work and go out with Jess afterwards, or just go home and watch Netflix. The next few weeks I was exiting my learning stage and was actually about to start my own investigations. We still hadn't cracked the burglary case and we were getting very busy.

After a couple months, I began receiving court notices for cases I assisted with. When we had court, it was usually scheduled when we worked mornings. After court, we were required to go back to work and finish our shifts. Going to court wasn't bad, it gave me the opportunity to see officers I hadn't seen since the academy. I drove downtown one morning to the Criminal Justice Center for a minor Disorderly Conduct hearing. When I parked my car, I began walking up 10th Street towards the CJC. As I entered the CJC, I got on the elevator to go up to my floor. These elevators were always packed because everyone gets on them including officers, attorneys, victims and defendants. It wasn't really safe for officers to be on the same elevators as defendants, but the courts could care less. The particular elevator I got on was jam packed, but with mostly officers.

I looked over in the corner and someone happened to catch my eye. He was tall and handsome. He was leaning back on the wall in the corner of the elevator. My eyes were stuck on his very masculine features. It started with his chest, which poked out with bulkiness through his fitted shirt. His shoulders were broad and he had the physical build of an athlete. His slightly tanned skin brought out the green in his eyes and the auburn color of his hair. He had a freshly cut fade on the sides with a classy hairstyle on the top of his head. He had a long beard, which was trimmed perfectly. He looked like he was fresh out of GQ magazine. His green eyes wandered around the elevator, looking at all the different people who were on with him. They wandered right in my direction and seemed to lock on me once he got a glimpse. I had his attention and he had mine.

For a second, I forgot where I was. As the elevator stopped on different floors, the elevator began to clear out and we maintained our eye contact. I gently brushed the hair away from my face, so he could get a good look at my beauty. He leaned up off the wall and I just knew he was going to approach me. He began walking towards my direction and I held my breath, wondering what he would say to me. Suddenly he stopped in his tracks and waited at the elevator door. The elevator got to the 7th floor and he got off. When he got off, he looked back at me in the most seductive way.

I had to get off the elevator and figure out who that guy was. I got off at the next floor and took the stairs back down. Once I got down to the 7th floor, I began looking around for him. He was nowhere in sight. It would have been impossible for me to look through every single courtroom. I peeked in a few rooms, but he wasn't in any of them. I decided to give up on my search and go back upstairs to the 10th floor. When I got into my courtroom, the prosecutor informed me the defense attorney was granted a continuous. That meant I was free to head back to work. I got on the elevator and started to call Jess, to see where she was. I wasn't really paying attention to floors and suddenly the doors opened. I looked up and he walked on. It seemed like a scene from a romantic love movie. I couldn't help but smile so hard when he looked at me.

"So, we meet again."

"Yes we do."

"I'm Luke."

"I'm Erica. Nice to meet you, Luke."

I saw his eyes glance down towards my badge, which was attached to my belt.

"Wow, you're a cop?"

"Yes. I'm a detective, why are you surprised?"

"Oh, because you're so-" he started saying before I cut him off.

"Let me guess, because I'm so short?" I said with an attitude.

"Beautiful. I was going to say I never saw a cop that looked this good before."

I began blushing and was enlightened by his obvious good taste in women.

"So why are you down here? Are you an attorney or a criminal?"

"Neither," he replied. "I came down here to appeal a traffic ticket, but they withdrew it."

"So you are a criminal."

We both laughed and he stated, "Only if you're the one locking me up."

I suddenly started getting hot. Everything he was saying to me was so perfect. He was so perfect. Just as we both started getting comfortable, the elevator stopped in the lobby and it was time to get off. We both exited the elevator and went outside.

"So where are we going for breakfast Erica?"

"Breakfast?" I asked while I laughed. "Since I don't know you Luke, I'm going to go right over there to Dunkin Donuts for a coffee. I don't know where you're going."

"Ouch, a dagger right to the heart," he said. "Well enjoy your coffee, Detective. Maybe I'll see you around." He started walking away and I was somewhat surprised. I didn't expect him to give up that easily.

"So that's it?"

"Yup. I'm not into the playing hard to get type."

So stupid. I went looking for this man and now that I had his attention, I was ruining the moment.

"Wait," I yelled and ran over towards him. "So where should we go?"

"I'm not in the mood for breakfast anymore, maybe we can do dinner one night," he said as he handed me a business card.

It was his business card and it appeared that he owned a lounge downtown. I couldn't believe I just messed that up.

I returned to work and told Jess all about Luke. I told her how handsome he was and how I almost ruined it with him. She laughed so hard at me, which made things worse.

"So let me get this right. You complain all the time about these cops that are always hitting on you, but you mess up the one chance you get with a hot guy."

"Basically."

Watching her laugh so hard made me laugh.

"Well I didn't mess up all the way. I did walk away with his business card."

“Business card? What kind of business does he have?” she asked. “He owns a lounge on Sansom Street, downtown.”

“Oh yes. We’re definitely going.”

“Oh, are we?”

“Yes. Tonight.”

“No. I don’t want him to think I’m desperate.”

“Girl, you are desperate. If he looks as good as you claim, you better go down there and make a better impression on him,” she said.

I thought about it and decided we were going to go down to the lounge. It was either that or stay home and watch Netflix on a Friday night. Throughout the entire day, all Jess talked about was going to the lounge. It seemed like she was more excited about it than I was. It was probably because I had already been rejected by Luke once and was nervous that it would happen again. I was still working on the commercial burglary case and I had no leads at all. Every investigator I contacted regarding the string of burglaries had the same exact information as me and no witnesses. If we planned to catch these suspects it was going to take a ton of hard work or a miracle. I continued working on the case throughout the remainder of the shift. I documented the times the suspects were in and out, as well as the exact tools they stole. It wasn’t long before the shift came to an end and Jess was in my ear about our plans for the night. After work, we went shopping for outfits and got our hair and nails done.

That night we went to Luke's lounge. It was a stunning venue. There was gorgeous lighting, beautiful women and of course, very good-looking men. I spotted Luke by the bar talking to the bartender and I quickly pointed him out to Jess. She was very impressed.

"Girl, you let that fine specimen of a man get away from you? You must be crazy."

At that moment, I totally agreed with her. He looked spectacular. He was dressed very classy and you could tell he was comfortable in his environment. I watched as different women continually approached him, just begging for his undivided attention. Jess and I walked over to the bar to continue checking out the scenery. As we got to the bar, I slightly brushed against Luke's arm as we walked by him. It was just enough to get some sort of response out of him. Jess and I sat at the bar and ordered two apple martinis. As we sat and waited for our drinks, I felt a strong presence approach me from behind.

"Well look who it is." The sound on Luke's deep voice echoed in my ear.

I took a deep breath in, catching a whiff of his brute cologne that covered the air around me. I turned around with a pleasant smile on my face and once again, I was left in a trance staring in his deep green eyes.

"I'm glad to see you came out."

"Yes, it's very nice seeing you again," I said, as I stood to my feet.

I wrapped my arms around his neck, initiating a very tight hug.

"Well someone is in a much better mood."

I ignored that statement and introduced Luke to Jess.

"Luke I want you to meet my good friend, Jessica."

Luke extended his hand to give Jess and handshake and she quickly stated, "Oh no, I need a hug too."

Next thing I know, Jess was hugging on Luke as if she had known him for years.

"Please tell me you have a brother that is just as handsome as you," Jess said to Luke.

He chuckled and replied, "I do have a brother. His name is Donny but unfortunately he is a married man." Jess had sucked her teeth and Luke said, "But I do have a cousin. He's up in the VIP lounge. I'll introduce you to him."

"Oh please do," Jess replied. The bartender made our drinks and Luke told us they were on the house. Luke put his arms around us and gave us a little tour of the lounge. I loved it. It was upscale and very classy. As we strutted through the lounge with Luke, I noticed we were getting side-eyed by everyone in attendance. Most of the men were checking us out, but the women were clearly envious. That made me want Luke even more. He led us over to the VIP section where we sat at a table full of food and bottles of liquor. There were several people in the section and Luke called one man over. The man that walked over was just a handsome as Luke, but with blue eyes. I was very impressed.

"This is my cousin Kyle," Luke said.

Kyle shook my hand and his grip was so strong and firm. He was definitely an all-around attractive man. Jess hopped right up and hugged Kyle, when he attempted to shake her hand. All four of us had a great time that night. We were eating, drinking and getting to know each other better. Jess and I were very impressed. We found out that along with the lounge, Luke owned a couple car dealership and was planning to expand to another lounge in New York. Kyle ran the dealerships and owned several storage facilities in the Tristate area, including one in Philly. We were in the presence of two very successful and handsome men. Throughout the night, we were introduced to many people. We were dancing with the men and we were the life of the party. We mingled with other women in VIP who tried to get our host's attention, but it didn't work. They seemed to only be worried about us and I loved it. We were in the lounge all night until it closed at 2:00 am. Being in the lounge was a much better experience than being at the FOP Lounge where we were treated like pieces of meat that every guy wanted a piece of. Tonight we were the two gorgeous women that every man knew they couldn't have. We stuck around the lounge until the employees finish cleaning up and it seemed like an entirely different place when it was empty. There was beautiful art on the wall and decor throughout the interior. All of that went unnoticed when the building was packed. I was very tipsy and the men were making us laugh. Luke decided to tell Kyle the story of me rejecting him outside the courthouse.

"That was the first time in my life I was ever rejected and all I wanted was some breakfast," Luke said.

"Wow, you must be a special young lady because I never saw my cousin give any woman a second chance," Kyle told me.

"I had to fight for this second chance because your cousin made me chase him all over Center City," I replied.

We all started laughing over the story because it was funny how we both exaggerated our own versions of what happened.

"Well how about we all go get some breakfast right now and that will make up for the courthouse rejection" Kyle suggested as he continued laughing.

We all agreed and headed to a diner in the Northern Liberties area. We walked outside and the men agreed to drive and we left Jess' car parked in front the lounge. We walked into a parking garage, where two attendants brought the cars. They were two BMW

I8's. Luke's was black and Kyle's was white. They were very nice cars. I looked over at Jess and she looked like a kid in a candy store. She was ecstatic and I felt like they were too good to be true. We got into the cars and headed to the diner. During the ride, I received a text message from Jess.

Jess: *I'm in love.*

Me: *Me too. Lol.*

Jess: *Kyle is sooooooooooooo fine.*

Me: *So is Luke ;)*

Jess: *I owe you big time*

Me: *No you don't. It was your idea to come down here. Great decision.*

I couldn't help but laugh because Jess was so silly. We got to the diner and ate well. We didn't leave out of there until 4:00 am because we were still getting to know each other. After we were finished, Luke and Kyle drove us back to the car to wrap up the night, although it was technically morning. I can't even explain how happy I was that I finally found the right guy and Jess possibly did to. We planned to go back to the lounge the next week, but I planned to see Luke before that.

I set up several dates with Luke and we really hit it off. He seemed so impeccable and was the perfect gentleman. I could not figure out why this man was not taken. The only reasoning he gave for being single was that he was a "complicated man to deal with."

I believe his exact words were, "It's easy to get my attention, but hard to keep it."

That stuck in my head because I was undeniably up for the challenge. I mentioned to Luke that we wanted to stop by the lounge the upcoming weekend to celebrate Jess's birthday and he was more than happy to have us. He said he would also try to make some arrangements for us to make it special. Luke was definitely a man of his word because up until the day of her birthday he kept me informed about the arrangements. I invited a bunch of people we worked with, so they could be there once we arrived. Jess was too excited about her 30th birthday and she invited a bunch of her girlfriends out to go with us to Luke's lounge. I texted Luke to let him know we were on our way and told him we were coming with friends. When we got to the lounge, it was lights, cameras and action. A red carpet was rolled out when we pulled up and a photographer snapping pictures. It was all unexpected.

Luke surprised us and made the whole night about Jess. When we walked in the lounge, the DJ gave Jess a birthday shot out and everyone inside was wishing her a happy birthday. Even complete strangers were greeting her and giving her hugs. If you didn't know any better you would have thought Jess was some sort of celebrity. One of the servers guided us to the VIP section where there was a whole set up just for Jess' birthday. This included Kyle who greeted her with a big hug, lifting her in the air. Jess was so happy; she began pouring tears of joy. Her girlfriends were very impressed and our coworkers were coming up to us and complimenting everything from the venue to the men by our sides.

Our section was full of hot men because Luke and Kyle invited a few of their friends to entertain ours. Although the section was full of men, I could see all the women still checking out Luke. He noticed this and made sure I knew he was all mine. He came over and had me sit on his lap while the servers brought out a dazzling birthday cake for Jess. After cutting the cake, Kyle carried Jess over to the DJ booth and they let her get on the microphone to give out a little birthday speech. Jess began thanking everyone that came out and it literally seemed like we were in a scene out of a movie. It was a stunning night and I couldn't thank Luke enough for doing that for her. The night went by so fast and before we knew it, the party was over. We stayed after the employees left again, but this time we didn't head to a diner. Kyle and Jess were having an intense make out session on one of the couches in VIP, so I asked Luke to take me somewhere so they could have a little privacy. He took me to his office, which overlooked the entire lounge from a large window. I could see everything, including Jess and Kyle going at it like two horny teenagers.

"You look absolutely exquisite tonight," he whispered in my ear as he walked up behind me.

Once again, the intoxicating fragrance of his cologne spread through the air. It was something about Luke that was very mysterious and I liked it. I looked back and kissed his lips. I followed his eyes, which were glaring down towards the VIP section. I could see that Jess and Kyle were now having sex in the section.

"Wow, I can't believe she's doing that," I said, as I chuckled and walked away from the window.

Luke remained at the window, focused on the show Jess and Kyle were putting on. It was almost as if he was admiring them.

"Why can't you believe she's doing that?" Luke asked. "Obviously she's a woman who takes what she wants before someone else has the chance to take it from her."

I took that as a subliminal message towards me, insinuating that I didn't go after what I wanted when we first met. I walked back over towards Luke and stood in front of him, close enough that he felt my butt on him. I was determined to show him what I wanted. I felt his hand brush my hair to the side and his soft lips kiss my neck. His firm hands gripped my hips and pulled me closer to him, allowing me to feel his penis get erect. I literally felt him grow inch by inch. I was so horny, I could no longer resist. I wanted him right then and there. I lifted my skirt and exposed the fact that I was not wearing any panties and bent over. As I bent over, I looked down at Jess who was still riding Kyle. I heard Luke undo his belt buckle and unzip his pants. The anticipation of him being inside of my wet vagina was killing me and suddenly I felt him. His penis was so thick. I felt his width once he put the tip of his penis in me. He entered me slowly and my moistness made it easy for him to go deep. My hands were pressed against the window as Luke began to pump harder and faster. I jerked after ever thrust, while I moaned softly.

"Oh yeah, deeper," I said as I moaned.

Luke grabbed a hand full of my hair and pulled it as he continued pumping me from behind. My legs began shaking and I felt myself reaching my climax. After reaching my peak, I could no longer handle the strokes from Luke's thick penis any longer. My vagina felt so sensitive and my legs felt like noodles.

"I'm about to cum," Luke said as he slowed down his strokes and eventually exited my dripping vagina.

I got on my knees and began sucking his thick penis. It didn't take long before he shot his load down my throat. I looked up at Luke, who was staring at me devouring his penis. I swallowed every drop of him, leaving him stuck just staring at me. I pulled my dress down and Luke pulled up his pants.

"That was really good."

"Yeah it definitely was," Luke said and he walked over to hold me.

It felt so good being in his arms. We laid down on a couch he had in his office and ended up falling asleep together. The next morning Luke woke me up and I was all smiles. He was definitely the man I didn't mind waking up to. We went down to the lounge area and found Kyle and Jess cuddled up. They were still half-naked and were sleeping like babies. I was kind of impressed looking at Kyle's naked body. We woke them up and they got dressed. Jess and I went back to her apartment.

"Oh my god! Thank you so much. That had to be the best birthday party ever," Jess said.

"I can't take all the credit. Luke did all that."

"Well, I need to thank him the next time I see him."

"Let's go back to there tonight."

"Why? So you and Kyle can do the nasty again," I said jokingly.

"You saw us?'

"Yup we were watching ya'll from his office."

She laughed and said, "Well I hope you two enjoyed the show."

"We actually did. It inspired us to put on our own show."

"Oh really. Well I would have loved to see that."

We laughed and talked up our experiences with both men. Jess and I partied hard and had so much fun; it felt like we were living in a fantasy. We were starting to become very well known in the lounge and the nightlife became very addictive. When we were at work, we weren't the main attractions so the nightlife scene was more comfortable for us. I agreed to go back to the lounge with Jess and we spent the rest of the day catching up on some sleep.

That night we headed back to the lounge, but our men were not there. Although Luke wasn't with us, we received the same treatment as if he was. The bartenders kept the drinks flowing all night. I texted Luke to let him know we popped up at the lounge to see him. We partied all night long and the men finally arrived to the lounge. We all were dancing with each other. I took turns dancing with Luke, Kyle and Jess. We left the lounge a little early and all went back to Luke's condominium. He was looking so good and I was all over him. Jess and Kyle were all over each other too. I told Luke I wanted a drink and he went into the kitchen and brought out a bottle of Patron. We all began taking shots and we decided to put some music on. We were having a great time drinking and dancing, when Jess looked outside and saw the pool.

"I want to go swimming. Erica, come on. Let's go swimming."

I could tell all the liquor was talking for her because she looked so drunk.

"We can't go swimming, we don't have bathing suits."

"Well I'm going anyway," she said. Jess walked out the rear door towards the pool, as she began undressing. I grabbed the bottle of Patron and followed Jess out to the pool. We took off all our clothes and got into the pool. We both were swimming around and giggling the entire time. My naked body felt good, submerged in the warm water. I was so glad Jess was with me because she made me feel so comfortable. Suddenly Luke and Kyle came walking out in their swim trunks. My goodness, you should have seen their bodies. They were both in shape and both looked amazing. We were two lucky girls. We all took a couple more shots of Patron and they both got in the water with us. The water glistened off Luke's shoulders and I just sat back and admired him. It was something about him that was very intimidating, which made my sort of shy. I was dipping in the pool, so that the water covered my body from my shoulders down. I looked over, watching Jess and Kyle enjoy each other's company. She was jumping in and out the water like dolphin, as they pretended to wrestle. Her loud laughter and playful personality, forced Luke's attention to be on her and not me. Jess was hardly shy as the water dripped off her exposed breasts. I even caught glimpses of her and Luke peeking over at each other. Those peeks quickly turned to looks and then flirting.

She began splashing us and said, "Ya'll need to loosen up."

She was right and I took another shot to do just that. I stood up in the pool exposing my cute body to Luke. He smiled and swam over to me like a shark that just found his prey. He remained submerged in the water and I felt his large hands wrap around my butt cheeks. That feeling made me giggle, which caused Kyle to look over towards us. I could see he was staring at my body and it was actually flattering. I now had all the attention. It was like a friendly competition between Jess and I, to see who got more attention from the men. Luke came up for air and Kyle asked him for the Patron.

I quickly grabbed the bottle and said, "You have to come get it" in a flirty manner to both men.

The next thing I knew, I had two incredibly handsome men swimming towards me. As they dove in the water, I threw the bottle across the pool to Jess and they didn't even know. I was pretending to have the bottle behind my back and suddenly I felt hands all over me. It felt so good to have them both all over me. It was very surprising and somewhat adventurous to me. A part of me wished Jess wasn't there, so I could have had that type of attention to myself all night. I felt hands gently grabbing my breasts and butt and I loved it.

As I was enjoying the moment, I heard Jess ask, "Hey guys, are you looking for this?"

She was holding up the bottle and suddenly they swam towards her. She threw the bottle back towards me and the next thing I saw was Jess being submerged under water. At that brief moment, it appeared as if I was the only person in the pool. Suddenly everyone reappeared for some air. Jess came up from the water moaning. I observed Kyle hugging her from behind and her hands gripping on Luke's chest. Kyle began kissing on Jess' neck and that made me wet.

I brought over the bottle and asked, "You still want some, Kyle?"

"Of course I want it," he replied in a sexy tone.

"Well, tilt your head back and I'll pour it."

Kyle dipped down into the pool and pulled me towards his body. He was so strong. As he pulled me close, his face was perfectly aligned with my breasts. He tilted his head back and stuck his tongue out. I couldn't help but notice how long it was. I poured a shot into his mouth and he kept his mouth open for another one.

"Let me pour it," Luke said.

I handed him the bottle and he walked up behind me. I felt the bulge from his penis pressed up against my butt. Luke kissed the back of my neck and slowly poured a shot of Patron down my chest. The cold liquor dripped off my nipple and into Kyle's mouth. His tongue was still out and I leaned forward slightly placing my hard nipple right on it. He immediately sucked on my breast. Kyle stood up in the water while our bodies were still pressed together and as he did, his hard penis got caught between my legs. I immediately moaned, reached back and grabbed Luke's head so he could continue to kiss on my neck. At that moment, as Luke was kissing on my neck, I felt a penis pressing up against my vagina and another between my butt cheeks. It felt absolutely amazing and I loved every second of it. I never had a feeling like that before. It wasn't long before Jess came over and joined in on the fun.

Jess swam over and immediately turned the tables by saying, "ok you two had your fun, now it's our turn."

I saw her dive into the water in front of Kyle and then he began to reach down. She was down there for about thirty seconds before coming back up with his swim trunks. She threw the swim trunks across the pool and took a second dive. This time I could see by the expressions on Kyle face, that Jess was doing something pleasant to him. His eyes glared in the water and he grinned while slightly moaning.

Jess popped back out the water once more for air, but this time said, "Erica, come here."

I swam towards her and we both took a dive. Once I was under water, the sight of Kyle's penis greeted me. It was nice. It wasn't as thick as Luke's, but it was much longer. I watched as Jess grabbed it and worked it in and out her mouth. While she did this, I grabbed a firm hold of Kyle's balls, which made him flinch. I couldn't hold my breath as long as Jess, so I quickly went up for air. As I did this, I looked up at Kyle's blue eyes that were an exact match to the color of the pool water. Gosh, he was so dreamy. He didn't say a word to me, he didn't have to. His blue eyes focused on my body and I took another dive to focus on his. This time I grabbed his long, hard cock and put it in my mouth. It felt like it was down my throat, but I continued sucking it. Once again, I couldn't hold my breath, so I came back up for air. I turned around and Luke was sitting on the pool steps, taking a shot of Patron. He was staring at us and enjoying the show. I went over to him and took off his swim trunks too. His thick cock was rock hard and I wanted a taste. I immediately began sucking him off. The pool water was splashing and he had his beautiful green eyes focused on me. After about five minutes, I saw his beautiful green eyes look behind me. I turned slightly and saw Jess coming over and Kyle following her.

"I want to taste," Jess said as she deep throated Luke's cock.

His hands reached down and grabbed our breasts, while we took turns sucking his cock. Jess began moaning as Kyle pounded her with back shots from the rear. I watched as his long cock went in and out her vagina, making it cream on every stroke. The echoes of her ass cheeks clapping against hips sounded lovely. This was turning me on and I wanted to watch for a while. I grabbed the bottle of Patron, which was almost empty, and took another shot. Jess had Kyle's cock in her vagina and Luke's cock in her mouth. She was one very lucky woman. I wanted to be in that position. I walked over and sat on Luke's hard cock. I slowly worked it into my vagina and unexpected moans captured the attention of Jess and Kyle. They were still fucking but it seemed like they were watching me ride Luke's cock too. As I rode Luke, I watched as Kyle maneuvered his hips side to side making Jess go crazy. Jess began sucking on Luke's balls as I still rode his cock. I looked backed and saw his eyes were closed he kept repeating "yea right there" and "shit." I knew it wouldn't be long before he exploded inside of me. I began riding him slow again, to feel his thickness inside of me. Jess' tongue was licking Luke's cock as my movements briefly exposed it. I watched as she licked his balls, looked up, and smiled at me. Suddenly her tongue went up Luke's cock and right to my clitoris. I went crazy because it caught me by surprise.

She began sucking on my clitoris while Luke's cock stretched me out and I couldn't take it anymore. I ejaculated so hard, it all literally came flowing out on to

Luke's cock, and Jess was still licking us. My legs began shaking and everything began spinning. I never had a feeling like this ever. Jess continued licking my clitoris and Luke kept stroking me, as I sat on top of him, lifeless. My body was so weak and I could barely hold myself up. Just as I was about to fall over, I felt a very warm sensation inside my vagina. It felt like a warm lube was squeezed in me. It felt sensational. At that moment, I knew Luke came in me. I was actually happy he came, because I was done and had no more energy.

I got off him, and watched as Jess and Kyle continued to please each other. I was floating in the water and I had the perfect glimpse of her riding him. Luke was also floating in the water and I couldn't tell if he was sleep or watching the stars. I don't even remember when Jess and Kyle finished up, I just knew at some point I was still floating and they were cuddling on a lounge chair alongside the pool. Luke was sound asleep in another lounge chair. The sun began peaking its way through the horizon and I finally swam out. My body was completely wrinkled from being in the water too long, but that experience was worth it. We all went inside and fell asleep.

After that night, things became very serious between Luke and me. We started dating and he even asked me to move into the condo with him. This was good because I was currently living in my parents' home. Luke treated me like a queen. I was living a very expensive lifestyle. From eating at five-star restaurants every other day, to driving Luke's luxury cars and taking countless vacations. Jess and Kyle dated for months too, but it ended because Jess had a very short attention span when it came to men. She had serious commitment issues and could never stay in a relationship. Although they broke up, they remained very close friends. We often hung out with each other, especially after I moved in with Luke. Jess and Kyle also took vacations with us. Things were so perfect and I had no complaints when it came to my love life. I couldn't say the same for things at work. The men at work would always joke around, saying we were too high maintenance for them and it was actually true. The good-guy personality didn't do a thing for me. I needed the mystery and thrills that Luke gave me.

It had been months and we were getting very busy at work. It seemed as if the crew from Lowes was back out hitting up stores again and they were racking up. They were stealing thousands of dollars' worth of tools and we had no idea what was happening to them. We had no leads on the tools, whether being sold at pawnshops or on the streets for straight cash. The Major Crimes Unit sent out bulletins about the burglaries and it seemed like this crew was on the radar of many police departments. I was actually doing well with my investigations and still helped William when he was working big cases. I remember around my birthday in April, William wanted me to assist him with serving an arrest warrant on a male wanted for a shooting near the Philadelphia Mills mall. This apparent premeditated robbery was a sneaker sale gone wrong. The alleged shooter led the victim to the area under the impression that he wanted to buy some sneakers from him, knowing his true intention was to steal them. William also had a search warrant for the house so our sergeant and some uniformed Patrol Officers responded to the house to assist us. The home was on the 3100 block of Magee Avenue and we had the front and rear of the house covered.

William knocked on the front door and another male answered. We announced ourselves and asked if the suspect was home, which the male claimed he wasn't. We began searching the home for the suspect, when I heard a noise in a closet. I went to open the closet and suddenly the door was pushed open on me. I fell to the ground and a shadowy figure ran from the closet towards the back door. William immediately began chasing him and he ran directly towards the officer's in the back. He was arrested along with male that answered the door and lied. We began searching the home for the gun used in the shooting and we hit the jackpot. Not only did we find that gun, but we also found several other guns and $50,000 worth of Crystal Meth. They were found in a cut out at the bottom of a mattress, located in an upstairs bedroom. Therefore, it seemed the suspect was into way more than just robberies.

We transported the suspects and the evidence back to the district. The suspect that answered the door went by the street name "Slim" and the alleged shooter went by the name "Ryder." Once we got back, we put them both in separate interview rooms and let them sit for a moment, while we processed the evidence.

"I can't believe we found all this stuff in that mattress," I said to William.

"I know, I definitely wasn't expecting this."

"So where do you think those two mongrels got the drugs?"

"My guess is that the Ryder kid probably robbed somebody for it all. The other kid looks too stupid to pull off anything. He reminds me more of an addict than a street guy," William said. "We'll see what each of them have to say once I start the interviews."

"Can I do the interviews?"

William gave me a look of doubtfulness and I knew what his answer was going to be.

"Listen Erica, if it were another job I would say yes but I really need to get some answers out of these guys. You didn't put that much time in on the street and you may not know the art of body language, deception and everything else that goes along with interviews and interrogations. So just sit in with me and stay quiet."

I was pissed, but I knew he was just being honest. I didn't want the fact that I wasn't working the streets for years, make people think I couldn't do my job effectively.

"Listen William, I want to help and I have to learn," I said.

"Ok well sitting in on the interrogation is learning," William said.

I smiled but in the back of my head, I was going to try to impress him. We walked into the room Ryder was in and sat down.

Ryder looked right at me and said, "Damn look at this little sexy bitch right here."

"Excuse you," I said. "Who do you think you're talking to like that?" I asked angrily.

"I'm talking to you, bitch."

"Fuck you asshole, that's why you're going to rot in jail from all those guns and drugs we got out of your house, you piece of shit."

Ryder started laughing and said, "You didn't find shit on me you dumb bitch."

"Well who do the drugs belong to? I know they aren't Slim's, so they have to be yours."

"Yo, get me a fucking lawyer and stop asking me all these dumb ass questions."

"Answer me. Are they your drugs? Are they your guns?"

Suddenly William jumped up from his seat. "ERICA, OUTSIDE, NOW!" he yelled with nothing but frustration. He slammed the door behind us and asked,

"What the hell was that? What the hell were you thinking?"

"I don't know. I just got upset."

"And that's exactly why you don't deserve to be up here. You didn't even work the street long enough to learn anything and that's why you let him get to you in there."

"But I-" I murmured as I attempted to speak.

"But nothing. Now we can't ask him shit. You just fucked it all up. I don't know who you called or fucked to get where you are today, but some of us actually work hard in this department and do things the right way."

"How dare you speak to me that way," I said. "You don't know me and you have no fucking room to judge me."

I stormed off and sat at my desk. I attempted to call Luke to tell him what was going on, but I overheard William ask another detective to sit in with him while he interrogated Slim. Although I was irritated with William, I wasn't just going to forget about the case. As soon as they walked in the room, I put my ear to the door to listen in and this is what I heard.

William: "Sir, you are under arrest for the crime of interfering with an official police investigation by lying to us and attempting to use deception to interfere with the arrest of your friend. You have the right to remain silent, anything you say can and will be used in a court of law. You have a right to an attorney and if you cannot afford an attorney one will be appointed to you free of charge. I want to ask you some questions about some things we found in the house today. Are you willing to speak to me about those things?"

Slim: "Yes I am, man. I'm sorry, man. I'm in big trouble aren't I?"

William: "That all depends on your level of cooperation. If you work with me, I will work with you."

Slim: "What do you want to know, man?"

William: "I want to know why you two had fifty thousand dollars' worth of crystal meth in a mattress."

Slim: "Aww damn, you found the meth? We're dead men."

William: "Why do you say that?"

Slim: "We sell the meth. We sell it for Ryder's cousin and he is bad news."

William: "What's his name?"

Slim: "I only know him by Buck, but he's the real deal. I heard Buck works for some very scary dudes. Like mafia dudes or something."

William: "So I guess it's safe to assume that Buck gave you two the guns as well?"

Slim: "Naw man. He gave the guns to Ryder. They don't trust me with guns, because you probably can already tell, I'm a user. I dabble in the meth and sometimes a little coke. That's how they pay me."

William: "What do they pay you to do?"

Slim: "Listen man, I think I already said too much. I'm going to be a dead man."

William: "Slim, you have to talk to me because you are facing a lot of jail time from the meth and the guns."

Slim: "Aww come on man, I can't go to jail man. What if I tell you something big?"

William: "Big like what?"

Slim: "Super big?"

William: "What is it?"

Slim: "No. First promise that I won't go to jail. I want it in writing."

William: "Listen, if the information is good enough, I will overlook the fact that you lied to me at the house."

Slim: "Promise me."

William: “I promise you, as long as the information is worth it.”

Slim: “Ok. So I’ve been watching the news and it’s been a crew going around stealing tools from a bunch of stores.”

William: “Yes I am very familiar with them. They burglarized one of our stores a few months ago”

Slim: “Well, that’s Buck and his crew.”

When I heard this my eyes got big. Finally, we had our first lead on the crew. I grabbed the folder off my desk with still images of the suspects from the Lowes footage. I stormed right into the interview room and William looked up at me with an arrogant expression on his face. I handed him the folder with the images and he spread them out across the table. Slim studied the photos as he quivered. It was obvious that he was coming down from whatever high he had earlier in the day. The interrogation continued.

William: “So you are telling me the suspects in these photos are the guys you are talking about?”

Slim: “Yea, I’m sure man. That’s Buck, C-4, Rimz, Vlad, Rell and Donny.”

William: “Where can I find these guys?”

Slim: “Man they’re all over the city. They don’t hang together often. I think they just do jobs together.”

William: “Well where can I find that van they’re driving?”

Slim: “You ain’t going to find it. The dude Donny has a cousin or brother that owns a storage facility, dealerships and a bunch of other stuff. They probably already sold that van and are using another one.”

OH MY GOD. I couldn’t believe it. I didn’t initially put two and two together. Donny had to be Luke’s brother, because I remember Luke mentioning that Kyle owned the storage facility I put my furniture in when I moved in with him. I ran out of the room and immediately called Luke, but he didn't answer. I went to my sergeant and told him I had to leave. I had to find out the truth. Was the love of my life a criminal? Was that the true reason he was at court when we met? Are his businesses even legitimate? I didn't know what to think. It got even worse when I walked to the parking lot and got into one of his luxury cars. I was caught up. I was sitting in a brand new Lexus, wondering if the man of my dreams was possibly involved in criminal activity. It couldn't be true. I was in so much denial. We lived together and I didn't see any of the stolen items from the burglaries or anything that would suggest Luke was up to no good. I could not get in touch with Luke and things were becoming urgent. I ran out of the district so I have no clue what else information Slim had been giving up. All I knew was I had to find out the truth and protect the man I love. As I was driving home, I received a text from Jess.

Jess: *Is everything ok? The sergeant told me you left work early.*

Me: *No everything isn't ok. I can't get in touch with Luke and he is in trouble.*

Jess: *What kind of trouble?*

Me: *Some serious shit. Can you try to get in contact with Kyle to see if he knows where Luke is?*

Jess: *Kk. Hold on.*

Jess: *No answer. What should I do?*

Me: *Nothing at the moment. I would like if you could stop by the condo later. In the meantime, keep an eye on the guy William is interrogating and give me any updates.*

Jess: *Ok.*

Once I got home, I waited around for Luke to get in the house. Hours passed and he finally arrived home.

"So where were you this entire time?

"I was out."

"Out with who doing what?"

He laughed. "Damn, I know you're a detective and everything baby, but why are you questioning me like this?"

I knocked over a lamp that was sitting on top of an end table and yelled, "Because my fucking boyfriend failed to let me know that he's related to a bunch of criminals."

Luke had a surprised expression on his face as if he didn't know what I was talking about. That made my blood boil because now was not the time for games.

"You need to tell me how involved you are in all these burglaries your brother, Donny, has been doing."

As soon as I said that, Luke avoided all eye contact with me and began looking towards the ground. That was exactly the confirmation I needed to realize he was involved somehow.

"Tell me now."

"Ok listen. I have nothing to do with the burglaries directly, that is all Donny and his crew. We get paid by some very important people to store the stolen goods, drugs and money at Kyle's storage facility. The only thing I do is handle some of the money and put it into our businesses to make it look legit. That's it baby, I swear."

As soon as he told me this, I broke down and cried. My emotions got the best of me and I was hurt. I knew everything was too good to be true and now I was living with a man who could possibly be going to jail.

"Why wouldn't you tell me this before we got serious?"

"Because we would have never gotten serious if you knew I was doing these things. I'm not a bad person baby, I just move money around for some important people."

At that time, I didn't know what to think or what to do. I had a choice to break up with Luke and have our department possibly arrest him and his family members, but that wasn't a real option for me. I stuck by his side a hundred percent and I had to think of how I could make these allegations disappear before they got back to Luke. Luke and I were in the house coming up with all types of crazy scenarios of what could happen and suddenly there was a knock at the door. The knock startled us because we weren't expecting anyone to show up to the home. I peeked outside carefully, while my heart was racing. As I pulled the curtain aside inch by inch, I saw that it was Jess and Kyle at the door. She must have left work early too. We opened the door and invited them in so we could all talk.

"So nothing much happened after you left. They made that guy give a written statement and William typed it up on his computer," Jess said.

"So who exactly is this guy that was giving a statement?" Luke asked.

"He went by the name Slim. He was arrested with a guy named Ryder earlier and he started giving up information to avoid jail time," I told him.

"I FUCKING KNEW IT," Kyle yelled as he clearly displayed his frustration. "I knew it was something weird about that little fucking druggy when I first laid my eyes on him. But Donny's boy Buck said he could trust that little rat."

"Well, what's happened can't be changed. He told everything, so whatever is in your storage facility that doesn't belong needs to go ASAP" I told Kyle.

"Yeah and you need to get in contact with Donny and tell him to tell his crew what's going on," Jess suggested.

As soon as I heard Jess' suggestion, I pulled her to the side.

"You don't have to do this. I don't want you to get involved in this nonsense."

"It's not a big deal, plus I'm not going to let you deal with this alone. No matter what happens you are linked to Luke and they will come for you too."

"So what should I do?"

"Just lay low and we will figure it out."

The rest of that night we spent trying to develop a way to keep Luke and Kyle off the law enforcement radar. I didn't even realize that what I was doing was an actual crime in itself. I just saw it as defending the man that I loved. I knew if anyone found out he was laundering money through his businesses, he would lose everything. We would lose everything. That night I laid next to Luke and began second-guessing myself. Did I truly want to risk all my family's hard work to get me into this career field? Did I want to throw the little integrity I had left away for a man? These questions kept me awake, preventing me from getting any type of sleep that night.

The next day when I went to work, everyone's focus was on Donny's crew. Slim's statement was more than enough evidence to start going after the crew, once they identified each member. The only good thing about the entire situation was the fact that Slim only knew everyone by their street names, otherwise they all would have been picked up by now. I approached my sergeant and inquired about the Lowes case. He informed me that the Major Crimes Unit was handling all the cases involving the crew and the Narcotics Strike

Force, FBI and ATF may be coming in to investigate the allegations about Kyle's Storage Facilities being a major drug stash spots. I knew if they were successful in doing that, they would immediately make the connection to Luke and then to me. As much as I wanted to help Luke, there was nothing I could do. It was no way the FBI and ATF weren't going to figure out everything that was going on. I loved Luke, but I had no way of fixing his problems. I had to text Jess.

Me: *I can't do it.*

Jess: *You can't do what?*

Me: *I can't help Luke. Sarge said the FBI is getting involved.*

Jess: *So what is that supposed to mean?*

Me: *That means there is nothing we can do to help them.*

Jess: *But he is giving you the world. You're just going to turn your back on him now?*

Me: *Yes. I have to. We have to. We have careers we need to focus on.*

Jess stop replying after I sent that last message. I know I was supportive of Luke in the beginning, but reality kicked in and I had to think about my future. What could I possibly do anyway to help him? It was too late. I had to make a decision and leave Luke. I had to get all my belongings out of his house, in case the FBI came knocking at his door. How ironic was it that I gravitated away from the "good guy" personalities and now I had to deal with a problem I wouldn't have if I dated a "good guy." I sat at my desk wondering what my next move was going to be, when my sergeant approached me.

"Erica, I need you to assist William with a follow up interview from a retail theft" he said. "He's tied up talking to Major Crimes right now and the woman that needs to be interviewed is in the lobby."

I had to find the previous interview from the woman so I checked William's computer. As soon as I got on it, I saw the interview with Slim was still up on the screen and a signed copy in the case file. I tried to ignore it, but I couldn't. I looked around and no one was paying attention, so I edited the statement. I changed Donny's name to "George" and changed the information about Kyle's businesses. After printing out a new copy of the statement, I forged Slim's signature and took the original statement. After doing this, I saw all the detectives running downstairs.

I ripped up the statement, threw it in the trash, and ran down to see what all the commotion was about. Everyone was standing around in the prisoner intake area and watched as paramedics carried a prisoner out on the stretcher. I looked closely and it was Slim. I was in a brief state of shock and I asked one of the officers what happened. He told me that the prisoner overdosed on some type of drug while he was in the cell. As soon as this happened, things were on lock down.

Supervisors were panicking trying to figure out how Slim was able to get drugs in his cell. The Major Crimes Unit was still on location and they quickly removed Ryder from the cell to transport him to their headquarters. Representatives from the FBI also responded to the location to begin an investigation with the supervisors on what happened in the cell area. All the detectives were ordered back upstairs to our desks. When we got upstairs, I observed William gathering all his information, including the statement to hand over to the FBI Agent. Everything was at a complete standstill at the district for about an hour. We were all left in suspense until the captain came upstairs to brief everyone on what was going on. This is what he said:

"Ok everyone, can I have your attention. As you all should know, there has been a crew going around committing commercial burglaries around the city and surrounding suburbs. We had no leads on the crew since recently, until Detectives Graham and Giordano apprehended two suspects that provided key information on the crew. Detective Graham was able to obtain a statement from one of the suspects, including the names of the crewmembers. Those names were cross-referenced with the FBI criminal database and matched the names of a crew of gun and drug smugglers, received from a confidential informant. This is why the FBI, ATF, Major Crimes and the Narcotic Strike Force were working together to take the crew down. They believe this crew is associated with the members of the Russian Mafia, which we all know have a very significant influence in Northeast Philly.

"Over the past year, the FBI connected the Russian Mafia to the Dougherty Family, which is led by brothers, Donny and Luke. The Dougherty brothers also strung along their cousin, Kyle, who the FBI had been tailing for quite some time now. About an hour ago, the suspect that was cooperating with our investigators overdosed on crystal meth in his cell downstairs. We are currently attempting to determine how he was able to obtain these drugs and if these drugs were distributed through the Dougherty crew. As of right now no one is to be involved in this case unless they have been specifically assigned by myself or a higher-ranking commander. All detectives are to only investigate cases that have been assigned to them by the sergeant. No one is to interfere with this particular investigation in any way. If you have any questions regarding anything I mentioned today, bring it to the attention of your sergeant. Thank you all."

I was panicking and could barely focus on my work. The FBI had been watching Luke and I had to let him know before it was too late. I called him several times, but he never answered the phone. I looked over towards Jess' desk, but I didn't want to approach her because everyone else was focused on their own investigations. I was so paranoid throughout the entire day. Once my shift was over, I went home but Luke never showed up. Things didn't seem right. I could not get in contact with Luke or Jess. I had a terrible feeling in my gut that something was wrong. I left the house and headed to the lounge, hoping Luke was going to be there.

When I pulled up to the lounge, I was suddenly surrounded by several black SUVs. Over a dozen Federal Agents jumped out of vehicles and ordered me from my car. I was terrified. My life had fallen apart. I was arrested and taken to the FBI building. Once inside the building, I was taken to a room that appeared to have already been prepared for me. I cried so hard and requested to make a phone call to my uncle, but I was denied. I was placed in the room and left alone. There were many files spread across the table and I began looking through them.

Inside were photographs from camera footage taken inside the district. The footage captured me changing Slim's statement. Once I saw this, I knew I was done. The photograph was time stamped and there were more that were taken around the same time. They were from the cell room and showed Slim's cell, just before he overdosed. I looked through the photographs from the cell area to see how Slim got the drugs. JESS. It was Jess. She was in the photographs walking by and briefly stopping at Slim's cell just before the overdose. It all made sense now. Once she stopped responding to my messages, she attempted to get rid of Slim herself. I opened another file and there were photographs of Luke and I out on dates and some taken in front of the condo. They were following him the entire time we were dating and neither of us knew. I was done and my life was over. All of our lives were over. I cried my eyes out in that room until two investigators walked in the room.

"Don't ask me anything because I have nothing to say to any of you. I want a lawyer," I said and the agents took me straight to their intake room to be processed.

Detective Erica Giordano was arrested and charged with interfering with a federal investigation. Detective Jessica Scorelli was arrested and charged with interfering with a federal investigation, tampering with evidence and other related charges. They were both terminated from the Philadelphia Police Department. Slim survived the overdose and continued cooperating with FBI. His cooperation was the key to the FBI's crackdown on the Dougherty crime family. Luke and Kyle Dougherty were arrested and charged with several federal drug, firearm and money laundering offenses. Donny Dougherty was arrested, along with the rest of his crew, and

charged with several burglary and related charges. Prosecutors obtained search warrants for everyone's phones and are using the phone records as evidence in the case, along with photographs and video footage. Everyone is still incarcerated and are currently awaiting sentencing hearings.

WATCH FOR THE NEXT
BLACK BADGE NOVEL

LIFE BEHIND BARS

Available Spring 2017

COMING SOON...

THE AFTERMATH SERIES - BOOK ONE
DESTRUCTION
NO GOVERNMENT, NO LAWS, NO ORDER
C.L. LOWRY

AMBUSHED
A SHORT STORY OF BETRAYAL
C.L. LOWRY

THE AFTERMATH SERIES - BOOK TWO
REVOLUTION
THERE IS A COST TO LIVE IN THE NEW WORLD... YOUR FREEDOM
C.L. LOWRY

THE
STRUGGLES
AND
SUCCESS
of SELF-PUBLISHING
The Simple and Understandable Guide to becoming a Self-Published Author
C.L. LOWRY

About the Author

C.L Lowry is a novelist and short-story writer, with no bounds. Along with writing suspenseful novels for mature audiences, he touches on current social issues in America. C.L. Lowry spent over five years in law-enforcement and uses his experience and education to demand his readers' attention with realistic scenarios throughout his stories.

C.L. Lowry was born and raised in Philadelphia, Pennsylvania.

If you have any questions, suggestions, complaints or want to volunteer as a beta reader and receive free advance-reading copies of new books, please email C.L. Lowry at CreedomPublishing@outlook.com. For more information on C.L. Lowry and book release dates visit www.creedompublishing.com.

Message from the Author

"We as a society need to get back to the days when we would help each other, instead of crucifying one another. The Black Badge stories are just a few of the problems people deal with on a daily basis. Whether it's financial hardship or drug addiction, there are people in this world that need help, support and love. If we work together, we can make the world a much better place."

Creedom Publishing Company

Creedom Publishing is a fully incorporated publishing company. Much like our slogan "The Home of Creative Freedom," we are committed to providing new and upcoming authors with the resources and opportunity to share their ***creativity*** with the world. At Creedom Publishing, writers have the ***freedom*** to make their own choices, without the burden of committing to one-sided contracts and guidelines that most traditional publishing companies offer. We are located in the Philadelphia area of Pennsylvania. Creedom Publishing also provides services for non-profit organizations, such as CrimeFighters Inc. and many more.

Our books are available for purchase on our site and eBooks are available through Amazon Kindle.

CONTACT THE CREEDOM PUBLISHING COMPANY AT:

CREEDOMPUBLISHING@OUTLOOK.COM

OR BY MAIL AT:

CREEDOM PUBLISHING COMPANY
P.O. BOX 1336
ROSLYN, PA 19001